Di Xin Emperor of Shang

(A Tale of Two Kings)

by Billy Ironcrane

Di Xin Emperor of Shang is a work of fiction set in remote history, and based in part on actual happenings. All incidents and dialogue, and all characters with the exception of some well-known historical figures, are products of the author's imagination, engaged fictitiously, and are not to be construed as real. Where real-life historical figures appear, the situations, incidents, and dialogues concerning those persons are entirely fictional and are not intended to depict actual events or to change the entirely fictional nature of this work. In all other respects, any resemblance to actual persons, living or dead, events, or locales is entirely coincidental.

Published by: Mc Cabe and Associates,
Tacoma, WA.
For permissions contact: billyironcrane@gmail.com

Illustrated by Renee Knarreborg
Cover Design Mc Cabe and Associates
Cover Art - "The Imperial Couple" by Renee Knarreborg

ISBN-13: 979-8-9926064-0-9
Library of Congress Control Number: 2025903020

To friends —
the real ones, flesh and blood,
always at the ready.

And to the good people of Ukraine,
Gaza and countless elsweheres
who have suffered needlessly.

Contents

Illustrations

*Di Xin
Emperor
of Shang*

Background

Our story begins with the Shang Dynasty (1600–1046 BCE), a civilization that flourished for nearly six centuries. During their reign, they made remarkable strides in mathematics, astronomy, and the arts. They developed a working lunar calendar and later refined a solar calendar much like our own. Their mastery of bronze weaponry and the composite bow made them a formidable force, while their craftsmanship in pottery, jade carvings, and funerary art left an enduring legacy. At the heart of their society was a deep reverence for Shangdi, the supreme ruler, with the king serving as his earthly intermediary.

For centuries, the Shang maintained their dominance, repelling threats from external tribes and internal rivals with relentless military vigilance. Their survival rested on the unyielding might of their armies, but such strength came at a cost. As war and expansion consumed their focus, hardship spread among the people.

At the height of their power, corruption and excess took hold. A succession of rulers governed with tyranny, sealing the Shang's fate. These vices came to define the reign of Emperor Di Xin, a once-brilliant leader whose rule spiraled into decadence and cruelty. His fateful union with Daji, believed by many to be a fox spirit in human form, marked a turning point that drew him ever deeper into depravity. Together, they sought to reshape the world in their own image—one ruled by unchecked power and ruthless domination.

But history spins like a wheel, whirring through cycles of cause and consequence. Tyranny breeds resistance, an inevitable reckoning. Di Xin's reign set forces into motion, unleashing a chain of events that challenged the very foundations of Shang rule.

Our story follows these events and the forces that propel the rise of King Wen and the emergence of Zhou, a once-isolated frontier community. A leader of vision and wisdom, Wen's steady hand lays the foundation for a new order—one he hopes will restore balance, peace, and prosperity to the Middle Kingdom. From humble beginnings, the Zhou ascend, poised to reshape history and usher in a new era.

"Ah, so much for character. When your very survival depends on whether you are breathing or exhaling in accordance with your master's dictates, where can your true character alight?"

The sage smiled, "Agreed! In these mad times, truth passes only between those deemed fools. Shall we be such fools, wielding our sabers of swamp straw? Let the wrongdoers lie, steal, and torment. We will defy them. Truth takes root in patience, which the arrogant lack. All will have their day, even the mad. And when chaos clears, what endures? Patience, compassion, dharma— and fearlessness. Ill-doers will gnash their teeth as their fleeting power crumbles, crushed beneath the very deceptions they once unleashed."

Middle Kingdom

Northern
Tribes

Changcheng

Huang He

Western
Wilderness

Wei He

Huang He

Yellow Sea

Zhou
Territory

Kingdom
of Shang

Yangzi Jiang

Yangzi Jiang

Eastern
Sea

Southlands

Guangdong

Zhuya
Commandry

Southern
Sea

Pearl Cliffs

R.Knarreborg v5 2024

Part 1

Di Xi—Emperor of Shang

Fish in the Stream?

By now, their eyes had fully adjusted to the soft glow. There's always a bit of wonder and enchantment associated with candles in snow caves. From within, one senses the universe outside, frozen, ominous, yet alive and aware. Stealing a glance from just outside the opening, its colossal eye pushes close, quietly surveying the delicate presence within. Given the simple elegance and peacefulness of their hideaway, the two rested and made their silent study. The only sounds, their breathing and the wind. Amplified by the vast quietude of alpine night. Eventually, they stirred. Mindful of keeping warm throughout the frosty night, Abbot Hui covered the portal with hide, knowing they would have to wake periodically to ensure the opening remained uncovered by freshly fallen snow. Suffocation always lay in waiting for the careless and the unwary. Many who trespassed from the east had already learned this to their regret.

Inside the shelter, heat from their bodies combined with energy trickling from the burning candles to provide ample comfort to where they could remove their outerwear and relax.

Bao Ling picked up the conversation.

"I want to thank you for sharing that[1]. A miraculous day for both you and Master Li. Heroes rising to their full stature and villains getting their just due. New friends flushed from where they had always been. There, but just beyond one's view. As though waiting to fulfill a purpose. There's great comfort in learning we are not alone in our toils. It's not always easy to believe others might be there. Ready and willing, waiting only for one's needs to show. Think about it. But for the situation, and the need, would they ever have made their existence known? Kindred spirits finding attraction of purpose in the sea of chaos, clinging tightly to the hope of finding righteousness and likeminded others. Then for a moment sharing common footing, and unlikely survival against all the odds."

Abbot Hui acknowledged with a silent nod.

"But what of the mace[2]? If I hadn't heard your account, I wouldn't have believed such a thing existed. How is it possible? Yet another evil, this one beyond words and imagination. Frightening in its scope, and accordingly, irresistible to those who would stop at nothing to achieve their aims. And what does it all say of me? Am I fit to judge? Can I be so different in my own constitution? How is it I lack even the slightest bit of understanding as to what motivates such behavior, yet thankfully find myself repelled by it?"

---

[1] Bao Ling is referring to Master Li's long-ago challenge made to the fabled Black Knight and the Knights of Wei. The full account can be found in our prior work, *Seed of Dragons*.

[2] The Assassin's Mace (Shāshǒujiàn). In Chinese lore, the grand-ultimate weapon, existing primarily in legends, and in the minds of power crazed despots. It possessed the capacity to neutralize any defense, and to gain dominance in every situation. You'll learn much more as we proceed.

"No Bao Ling. You understand it fine. You just don't do it; nor do you have it in you."

"What don't I have in me?" fired Bao Ling, ever mindful of those whose lives he had taken, now numbering more than he could count. That didn't come from innocence, or from fine intentions. At some point each day, he found himself questioning the tragedy of their loss against the practicality of his own survival. Guilt, regret, anxiety, anger. Always there — gnawing away at him from somewhere inside. For a moment, he saw himself as just another Black Knight in the wakening. He felt sure they had both started out the same way, shaped by experiences over which they had no control. Would something inside someday tempt him to turn? How would he find the will to resist?

"The willingness to surrender your humanity," answered Hui.

"I fear it's more complicated for me. Honestly, I don't know or trust whether I could stand up to temptation of such magnitude. What about you Hui? How do you see yourself?"

"I believe you could stand up to it simply fine, and I believe the same of myself. In fact, I know it for myself. Regrettably, out there it's different. I'm afraid the world would consider you and I to have flaws of character. Possessed with unfortunate weaknesses. Misguided concerns for what has no significance, and paucity of personal drive which brands us both to be inept, unambitious fools. Two men with talent enough to become powerful war lords, even more, but seemingly without one wit of the requisite desire. Times have indeed become very strange. Too many have diverted from life's true purpose and are quick to look severely upon others. A tragedy of epic scope and proportion."

"I understand what you're saying. You're hinting at what I've always considered my finest attribute."

"Explain."

"I seek quietude and calm with the same ferocity that others seek wealth and influence. My drive is no less requisite than theirs. I simply aim for a different spot on the range."

"Are you satisfied with that?"

"Would that I had them. Quietude, calm? No, they continue to elude me. And I continue to chase. Like a hungry dog. Yet even I'm not spared from diversion. The harder I push toward them, the more quickly they melt away. You're a monk. Isn't that how it is with your pursuit of the great awakening? If not this lifetime, the next, or the one after? The question always lingers, is this where I should be? If I had taken another path, could I have made things better, for myself, for others? I have no answers for this, nor am I able to say where righteousness should lead me."

Shi-Hui Ke laughed, then retorted, "I expect Liu Bei could have answered that for both of us. But considering what transpired, would we have accepted what he said? He stands even now as the embodiment of righteousness. His ambition to restore Han remains as the great historical undertaking, unselfishly dedicating his entire being to a single purpose. All gone! Even Zhuge Liang couldn't account for the failure, and he knew everything! Tragically, countless millions lost their lives in the interminable strife of three empires gone berserk."

Half joking, Hui continued, "As your self-designated spiritual adviser, I would counsel you not to judge yourself harshly Bao Ling. You and I, in some ways are like fish caught in a stream—without purpose, or direction, but always where we should be, always one with the righteous water, facing forward into the flow, never away. Anticipating whatever comes, ever ready to act. Those others, milling about like wild bear along the banks, take what they will, acting like they already own it all. Or eagles in the sky, scouring the terrain for whatever captures their fancy, then attacking ruthlessly. Where can anyone find peace in this mix? Never-ending, if not the one, then the other. We see the carnage and devastation, spared only because we slip about securely and unnoticed in our watery retreat. That's how it is for us, slick, slippery, clever and quick. Must we do more? Should we do more? Will it matter if we do?

I have no answers for you, except when we risk trying, we find ourselves instantly pulled from our element. That's the cost, a high price indeed. I will tell you this. I do what I do because I do it, and my objectives reflect simplicity itself. I seek to actualize who I am. I expect to experience freedom. I will oppose and repel who or whatever threatens my people, my family, me, my principles or my honor; just as I will do likewise for anyone who feels as I do and requests my assistance. That sets me square in everyone's sights. I would guess it's the same for you. You and I both move like water, ever fluid. It's a gift we have.

Thinking more about it, we're not at all like fish in the stream. A realization we should ignore? Simply another distraction? Might we be the stream itself? Rooting somewhere beyond the ability of our constricted consciousness to see or understand; raging defiantly toward a future gripped in chaos and uncertainty, sure of only one thing. The pure and fluid character of our medium, carving and shaping all, flushing the impediments and poisons, and leaving dharma restored in its wake. Could we be its trustees? Fish … now I say not! Just our thoughts swimming about in the eternal flow. To some, fish in a stream—to us, two men seeking to self-actualize, stuck for a moment in an illusion of frustration and limitation, soon perhaps to open into full awareness."

An Alliance of Necessity

"That would be nice."

"Would it? With full awareness comes great responsibility. Even Colonel Sun struggled to bear the burden. I've heard he was not a happy man when he finally decided to disappear."

"What do you know of his disappearance?"

Surprised, Hui asked, "Sying Hao hasn't spoken to you of this?"

"No, except only for how much he missed him. Nothing more, and I chose not to press him further. When the day comes for him to talk, hopefully I'll be there for him. What about you? How much do you know?"

"Well, there's not much to say. One day, Colonel Sun disappeared. They were like father and son. From the beginning, schemers in the Court jumped on the opportunity to question Sun's loyalty. They promulgated accusations unfit for repetition. With him gone, Sying Hao became their whipping post and the next target for their incessant plotting. It's like that. Always point the accusing finger at someone else to keep the flame from yourself! The sons of bitches couldn't risk having their true natures exposed. If ever that happened, they'd swing in the wind as traitors.

"Instead, they spread lies and poison. Pointing everywhere, cultivating fear and mistrust, a constant succession of insinuations. Absence of proof or substance in fact made no difference. Simple repetition assured the

spread. They bellowed 'Traitor! ... Scoundrel! ... Schemer!
... Liar! ... Cheater! ... Imposter! ... Pervert!' Trusted tools
from their war chest, meant to fabricate structures of deceit.
It's no different than some trickster playing his cup game at
the marketplace. Except the trickster is an honest deceiver.
Bending reality first one way and then the other. With utter
certainty and conviction, you pick this cup or that, fully
expecting to find the gold piece beneath. Always, you end
with nothing. Or perhaps a bit of fruit if he be a generous
deceiver.

For reasons inexplicable, charades like this work best on
those possessing princely power. The statelier they are, the
more gullible. The game was afoot everywhere in court,
even reaching into the imperial bed chambers. Could it be
the powerful become blinded by their own fears and
mistrusts, and the insecurity of their perpetual isolation?

"By then, the young officer Sying Hao had already
proven himself a great warrior. No one had the gall to take
him head on, or to risk the consequences of a failed
assassination attempt. Only a fool would cross him directly.
Then there was the matter of his stepping into the shoes of
the late minister Zhuge Liang, assuming many of his
deceased teacher's responsibilities. No one else seemed
either up to it, or if they were, decidedly couldn't tolerate the
heat. It happened unexpectedly. No one foresaw his quick
ascension to the role. For reasons beyond the apprehension
of all, it seems Emperor Liu Shan[3] had somehow grown to
trust the wise counsel of Sying Hao, as though to spite all the
carefully sown seeds of slander. Ignoring their objections,
and the flood of accusations, the emperor never questioned
his loyalty, to the detractors' great chagrin. They now found

---

[3] Son of Liu Bei. Heir to the throne of Shu.

themselves in a stalemate. Leveraged and fronted against an imperial partnership. Sying Hao somehow stabilized the failing empire and managed to hold the wolves of war at bay. This enabled the "fool" Liu Shan to orchestrate an eventual transition to Wei with what remained of Shu still fundamentally intact. He spared the people from unimaginable suffering.

"There were regents of course: Jiang Wan, Fei Yi, Jiang Wei and Liu Xuan. The first two were handpicked by Zhuge Liang himself, as his final days rolled to a close; the others selected by destiny. Jiang Wan and Fe Yi administered well, and Sying Hao worked in harmony with them, three independent men grounded in reality. Had their chosen courses endured, the kingdom might have persevered and survived independently of Wei and Wu. When Jiang Wan[4] and Fe Yi[5] passed, all went to hell.

"Sying Hao, though isolated, continued to hold the emperor's ear. The would-bes at court forever tied their malicious concerns regarding Sying Hao's loyalty to the mysterious disappearance of Colonel Sun. One day they accused him of duplicity with Sun in treachery — the next day of murdering his father, and the next of consummate manipulation, having skewered everyone in his path until emerging alone as a manipulative schemer firmly staked at the emperor's side. *An evil wizard more skilled than even Zhuge Liang,* they charged; never failing to mention in their next breath how Guan Yu, Zhang Fei, even the Tiger Generals had all met their ends, yet Sying Hao somehow remained. 'Didn't that say something?'"

---

[4] 245 CE

[5] 253 CE

Bao Ling observed, "How they all wished they could be him!"

Hui smiled, then went on. "Always, at the core of accusations, lay the mystery of Sun Wu Kong. What happened to him? At first, Sying Hao had no clue as to Sun's whereabouts. He thought about it constantly, agonizing over his seeming abandonment by the one whom he had come to regard as father. With Sun gone, he stood alone. Guan Yu, Zhuge Liang, Zhang Fei and many notable others were all departed. He had never imagined himself surviving the whole lot of them, but here he was. Years passed without a clue to Sun's disappearance and whereabouts. He had explored all possible leads and ran them to their empty ends.

"His relationship with Liu Shan surprised everyone, seeming to come from nowhere; then taking unexpected root and holding firm against all onslaughts. Unlike the case with his mentors Sun and Zhuge, who served Liu Bei, Sying Hao had no great love for Liu Shan. His situation brought to mind Red Hare[6] without Guan Yu; such had become Sying Hao's state after Sun's disappearance. Nevertheless, he continued to do his duty to his impeccable best, all the while heartsick and ever searching for his father and Master.

"That's not to say he held the emperor in light regard. Sying Hao eventually came to terms with the machinations at court, and fully understood how precarious had become the emperor's position. Without Sying Hao in proximity, the emperor would have been a dead man. More than once, Sying Hao single handedly foiled direct attempts at assassination. He never said anything of it, knowing it

---

[6] The fabled horse of Guan Yu, loyal to no other person. At Guan's passing the horse would serve no other, and simply stopped eating, until it passed.

would only trouble an already beleaguered leader. To be fair, Liu Shan first ascended as a child, following in the wake of a legendary father. Poor decisions, a weakened military, major defeats, the failure of the Northern Campaigns, even his father would have struggled to keep proper rein on the now fragmenting court with its sickeningly ambitious and ever scheming vassals.

"It's not clear to what degree Liu Shan confided in Sying Hao. Indisputably, their partnership averted disaster and skirted ruin. Soon enough, Sying Hao came to appreciate how even in his very delicate position as ruler, Liu Shan perpetually balanced one faction against another in what the astute Sying Hao deemed to be a consummate emasculation of Emperor Liu's rivals. Picking them off one by one from the flanks with a touch ever so delicate, no one even suspected who had guided the blade. Apart from token concessions, and sacrifices of regretful necessity, no internal foe or aspirant could gain traction on this forever deemed imbecile emperor. As he bumped around, smiling ingratiatingly, followed by his train of concubines, Liu Shan had them all tied in knots. It seems only Sying Hao knew the emperor's true nature. A fool he was not. That alone may be what in turn kept Sying Hao alive. So, in that sense, they were each in the other's debt. As you might imagine, plotters invariably demanded his removal, one way or the other. But the emperor had grown a new right hand, and he had no intentions of giving it up."

Looking for Center at the Temple

The next words from Hui caught Bao Ling by surprise.

"Which of course made it all the more difficult when one day, Sying Hao came to request his leave."

Bao Ling asked, "Why would he do that? Where else could he go to have impact?"

"That's exactly what Liu Shan said. It took some considerable reflection on his part, but Sying Hao had decided, evoking the example of his mentor, to leave the world of men. Who knows the intricacies of why? I suspect he tired of it all. He had invested enough time looking for answers there and had found none. Years had passed. The intrigue, the treachery, the incessant battles and the lunacy at Court. If only Sun had been there. They could have muddled through it together. But then again, Sun had long ago said the very same of Zhuge Liang, and where did that lead. For sure, Sying Hao tendered his explanations and rationales in responding to Liu Shan. The emperor said none of it added up, accusing there was more than what he chose to reveal, to which Sying Hao stood only in silence, unable, or unwilling to say more.

By then, the emperor had grown very fond of his First Counselor and valued his every word and thought. Because of that, he had a good inclination of when words were missing, or thoughts veiled. With Sying Hao gone, the royal surrounds would fill with assholes and usurpers. He knew there would be no safe harbor, even in his own court, and no replacement so trustworthy as this man to guard his back or blinded sides.

"By that time, the emperor had matured and wizened with age and experience. Not too long before, under Liu Bei's expressed directive, Zhuge Liang became Regent of the realm, responsible for directing and guiding affairs until the sixteen-year-old child-emperor achieved majority. Under the steady hand of Chancellor Zhuge Liang, order and integrity continued as the norm throughout the realm This was a man who did not particularly cotton to pricks and knew to deal with them summarily. The other kingdoms? Not so fortunate. Despite their great power, Wei and Wu had no one comparable to a Zhuge Liang, and accordingly, the threat of internal strife and turmoil played constant. Though still empires, generations of conflict had left them bare. Now, the only semblance of their once glorious civilizations clung to the safe harbors of their prominent cities.

There, the ruling power hung on the support of massive garrisons. Elsewhere, all lay pillaged or exploited to ruin. This was so, even in previously long-spared Wu. Once removed from the immediate purview of the ruling court, outlying regions fell to the charge of ruffians, warlords and thugs. Seeing these changes elsewhere, Liu Shan understood the profound influence of Zhuge's invisible yet ever guiding hand in the affairs of Shu, and he trusted him fully. The trust in Zhuge Liang never faltered, even when toward the end there had been allegations of the wizard's quibbling and arguing with demons and deities which no one else could even see. 'Offending even the heavens,' the accusers argued. To his credit, the emperor responded to the charges, 'If Chancellor Zhuge quibbles and argues with demons and deities, he is doing so for our benefit—and when he deems such necessary, he speaks for me.' The high ministers whispered among themselves, 'See how even the Son of Heaven has gone mad.' For added effect, and to keep the multitude of suitors in check, Liu Shan had one or two of the accusers boiled slowly in oil, proclaiming, 'Zhuge Liang and I are one; be sure you understand that. Always! Whoever accuses, slanders, attacks, or disregards Chancellor Zhuge commits treason and will incur the most severe consequences.'

"From the onset of their pairing, for the boy emperor, Lord Zhuge had become a second father. For their eleven years together, until the wizard passed, it remained ever so. No less than an imperial funeral marked the degree of loss to the nation and to the ascendant ruler. The emperor walked alongside the funeral train, hand on casket, wailing inconsolably, himself a trumpet for the collective anguish of his people. Then, like Sying Hao, Liu Shan grew to know the true depth and reach of individual solitude and isolation. Neither of the two would have wished it on anyone but could not deny in themselves. It had become their common lot. Why, at times they even joked about it to one another, if only to briefly lighten the constant weight upon their spirits.

"Few details remain providing insight into Emperor Liu's predicament. History has recorded nothing of his doings, his undertakings, or his achievements. Surely, he was there for a reason, and we prefer to think he was the best man for the job, but who can say? Zhuge Liang was dead. Though Liu Shan never let go of his hope, or even his faith-rooted anticipation, Zhuge Liang did not resurrect, or return to the living. Not ever!

"No less hopeful for the return of Colonel Sun, Sying Hao half-expected his own visibility at court would ensure

Sun could readily find him, when and if the time came. Regrettably, we have no record of such ever happening."

Surprised at this revelation, Bao Ling asked "Then Sun is truly dead?"

"No, we in the mountains do not believe so."

"What then?"

"I have no easy answer for you. What I know is at some point, in the lull between campaigns, Sying Hao took a respite from court and came to Crystal Springs Temple. He came alone, our people knew him well and greeted him warmly, surprised in fact at how little he had aged over the years since they had last seen him. He had understandably gained much in his apprenticeship to Zhuge Liang. Might that have included Zhuge's own insights into the secrets of immortality? That's what some among us thought.

"He asked to take retreat at the temple, explaining he felt his spirit had drifted from native alignment and the malady had grown beyond his ability to resolve alone. He needed our help. To those who knew how to see these things, he had diminished considerably from his affliction. Clearly, his never-ending fretting over Sun had taken him off his mark, and befogged. How does one get back? They say it seemed like he was there, but he wasn't. Like a ghost, he was forgetting who he was. Talking to himself. The Shu people were delighted to help him of course. His friendship and support stood long true and unwavering, despite the travails and the times. It would be an honor to render service in return to his need."

"What did he do there?"

"He meditated; and then he studied the murals[7]; and then he meditated some more; and then again studied the murals, a cycle which went on for months."

"… and?"

"… and … and nothing. It seemed this routine would wind round forever. For him, like a prayer wheel. Our elders grew sorely concerned, seeing how a great friend of our people had somehow gotten confounded and hopelessly mired in life's trickeries. They invited him to meet and discreetly conference with them. There, he freely admitted he had indeed gotten stuck, saying he had looked everywhere for answers to questions he didn't even know how to ask. There were no leads, no trails. He had hoped for a loose thread or even a crumb. Something to encourage his continued pursuit of the now seemingly impossible goal. Or to free him to abandon it before it did him in."

"What impossible goal could that be?" they asked.

Hui emphasized, "Remember who we're talking about here. Sun Wu Kong. This isn't a guy who goes around unnoticed for long."

Sying Hao replied, "I must know what happened to father Sun. My spirit will not have peace until I do."

"The darkness and lines beneath his eyes told all. Even the monks grew concerned he had not been sleeping. The elders empathized with his suffering. They too had learned of Sun's disappearance, just as they had caught wind of the terrible things said of him by the liars at court. He had long ago become part of our people's collective spirit. So, after some deliberation they uniformly agreed to hold a ceremony

---

[7] Artwork, attributed to Zhuge Liang and his disciples. Found on walls virtually everywhere within Crystal Springs Temple.

elevating his ties to the Shu tribe. A formal memorial enacting traditional rights marking his adoption into the community."

"Ceremony?" questioned Sying Hao, "I wasn't aware of it. When did this happen?"

"The elders explained how Sying Hao was not the only friend who had retreated to the temple hoping to restore his center; just as he was not the only one to painstakingly study the murals while doing so."

Sying Hao felt as if a charging Red Hare had struck him senseless. "What do you mean? Who came before? When?" he asked.

"Why, Colonel Sun," they answered in unison. It was as if they anticipated the question. They even smiled as they said it. Indeed, he suspected someone had coached them into saying it exactly as they did.

"Hearing that, Sying Hao fired a stream of questions, intent to learn more and to extract every detail no matter how minute or seemingly insignificant. Collectively, it turned out they knew nothing beyond what they said, except that Sun had come sometime after the passing of Zhuge Liang. They learned of his puzzling disappearance not long after he departed Crystal Springs and returned to Chengdu. It bewildered them."

Sying Hao pushed them for detail, "I don't understand. Was there something he learned? Did anything happen?"

"He looked around the group hoping, expecting someone to have an answer. Glancing about, he encountered only blank expressions and shrugs of resignation.

"Sying Hao had wanted for more, but that was it. There would be nothing else. They had given all they could. Seeing his pained expression, the elders looked politely away, their compassion leading them to conclude they had failed to ease his pain."

God's Don't Read Minds

Then, after some long pause, Sying Hao's face lit. *"They all knew to say 'Colonel Sun' when I asked the question. It's as though they expected I would come, and to anticipate my asking the question. Someone led them to expect me, to help if they could, and to say what they said when they said it, and nothing more. In their exuberance, they couldn't even suppress their smiles as they discharged their final duty sealing the message in their unison. Colonel Sun's hand in this is indisputable."*

Abbot Hui continued, "He knew then to press no further. Both Zhuge and Sun made sure he too understood one thing above all. What happened among the three of them was none of the god-damned gods' business. Accordingly, he would invoke the elders of Shu no further, lest they say and reveal too much. He smiled politely and thanked them profusely. Something had happened, a discernible change. What unfolded impressed the Shu elders. He had entered confused and lost. Now he would be leaving renewed and assured, but most importantly, centered and re-integrated. They regarded the transformation in quiet wonder.

"Why so? Because now, though still embedded in chaos and uncertainty, he knew one single thing with absolute certainty. His father had not abandoned him! The tables had turned. The elders were now the ones riddled with confusion. What had they said that so changed things for Sying Hao? Did their not having more to offer even matter? No, for them a friend had regained hope and no longer bore the anguished look of a lost man. They could only savor the moment and be satisfied for their part. Their own spirits lifted quickly as well."

Elsewhere, in the heavens, the gods paused suddenly from their customary machinations. They took careful notice of Sying Hao's reaction. Something about it drew their concern. Why did Sying Hao have such a profound change in demeanor? It looked as if a crushing weight had lifted from his shoulders. They could not fathom; and they didn't like how that felt.

In the far future, the children of Shu and their children's children would sing songs commemorating the day Sying Hao regained his center.

It would turn out to be that important.

Do you wonder about it? What caused the change in Sying Hao? The elders hadn't really said much to him. Yes, Sun Wu Kong had made his own pilgrimage to the retreat without telling anyone, not even his adopted son. He came, he meditated, and he carefully studied the murals. Then he went. They were, after all, the embodiment of Zhuge Liang's essence. They preserved all which remained of the great wizard's consciousness. For Sun, like having a friend come back for a needed conversation and revisiting old times. Sun never forgot their last meeting; it played ever in his thoughts. Even when the burden of sorrow sometimes made him wish it would stop; quickly offset only by the fear of further loss to him if indeed it did.

The wizard had devised a plan to end chaos, which by then both Sun and the wizard knew to be the handiwork of the gods. In his backhanded way, the wizard had all but said as much. As to the plan, he could not share it openly, nor could he record it or give overt instructions. You may recall from what you learned. The gods knew everything, except what remained within our own thoughts. Their powers, great and penetrating as they might be, could not reach to see into our innermost sanctum; nor could they preclude the freedom of our own will from acting upon them. Sun understood this well, a lesson gleaned over an eternity of experience. The gods will smile and court you, lay their divine arms over your shoulder, or warmly take your hand, then ask you to speak openly about what's troubling you and pledging things would turn for the better. They'll even do a thing or two to prove their empathy as they dig deeper, looking all the more closely for what might yet lie hidden from their view. Give that up, and you become expendable. No different than a Black Knight without his mace[8]. Could it be this singular freedom within each of us, somehow threatened the gods?

You already know about their issues; we've talked of them elsewhere. They cling to eternity and see endless time as their exclusive domain. They must live! Forever! For them, any other living thing with potential constituted a threat to that objective. So, they wreaked their havoc incessantly, trusting chaos over all virtue as the means to accomplishing their self-serving ends.

Sun made certain Zhuge had learned this lesson well in their long time together. At first, Zhuge had rejected these blasphemies, clinging to his innate trust in the gods. "Who but them can help us?" But when he saw the reach, pokes, and thrusts of their invasive hands and their fickle fingers wriggling about and stirring the interminable troubles plaguing mankind, he soon enough realized the merit of Sun's reservations. Later, while serving as counselor to Liu

---

[8] When the fabled Black Knight lost the Assassin's Mace, he lost all status at court and wandered aimlessly until his end.

Bei, the weight of their prying plagued his very existence. He countered, parried, and maneuvered as best he could in his dealings with Wei and Wu. It was only when Lord Liu passed that Zhuge Liang saw the hands of the gods now reaching into everything. If this continued, there would be no basis for hope. Humankind would fade. He re-directed his sights, now making them his ultimate and final focus over the course of days he had remaining.

Sun Has a Dream

He could afford no miscalculations on this. In the time remaining, nothing would distract him from his purpose. When Zhuge Liang first assumed the role of regent, what little record exists shows he banned the position of official historian at Liu Shan's court. He would never again leave trails or leads for the eavesdropping deities. Even after he passed, Emperor Liu Shan chose to honor his will, maintaining the ban for the entirety of his remaining rule. Perhaps the wizard clued him in to the underlying reality. Regardless, for that very reason, few specifics exist as to the substantive nature of Liu Shan's reign. It is also possibly for that same reason that scholarly histories written in later times record him to be a fool. What do they know?

This, we do know. Zhuge Liang would not have tolerated a fool for so long.

So, Sun knew his wizard friend had been on to something, just as Zhuge's earthly end neared. At best, it had seemed to all effects a losing race against time. He also knew his friend would never give up the fight for righteousness and order, even with death rapidly losing patience in its waiting. Still, the wizard revealed nothing to him. No blueprint; no guide; no pointers; no words. Just a parting reference to something he had found, something of which he never spoke of, since, if he recklessly shared it to others, it would be known also to the gods, and would then come to naught.

When Zhuge passed, Sun at first despaired. In recent years, all their combined efforts had started to come unglued. His eternal eye glimpsed the end of mankind fast approaching on the horizon. He agonized over it. What did Zhuge Liang know that he couldn't tell?

From within the depths of his darkest despair, one night Sun Wu Kong had a dream. Who's to say about messages in dreams? Are they just us? The ancestors perhaps? Mind you, Sun had none. Ghosts of friends, acquaintances, loved ones? Were the gods privy to what we learned from them? Who knows?

I would say, apparently not. Sun had his dream, and they didn't have a clue as evidenced by their glee in his subsequent continued downward spiral into lunacy. Which we know now to have been just another of his transformations. Perfectly executed.

He dreamt of Zhuge Liang. It proved to be a comforting dream. Sun had been walking alone, it seemed endlessly; for time had stopped in the astral world. There, at the end of a long trail across an empty, sun-baked expanse, stood a solitary boulder. A monolith in a sea of sand. Only when Sun neared did he see his old friend sitting atop, not unlike the mystics he had encountered long ago in the high western mountains. Zhuge was young again, much like he had been when they first met. His warm smile left no doubt he had been waiting patiently for his friend's arrival. On sighting him, an overjoyed Sun hurriedly closed the gap, running with the speed of wind until nearing the base, when Zhuge held his palm high signaling him to stop. He did, and just as he was about to call the wizard's name, Zhuge's raised palm turned about and covered his mouth, leaving no doubt there were to be no words exchanged. Sun stood, momentarily at a loss. Then he fought the impulse to smile, his friend had learned well, leave nothing for the ears of the gods. Not even in the realm of dreams. They stared at one another resolutely, then Zhuge Liang reached with his right hand, turning completely about and sighting over his right shoulder. He then extended and pointed his fore and middle fingers into the distance.

He looked back to Sun, who understood completely.

He must continue his ordained path and search for what his wizard friend now signaled was for certain waiting … somewhere out there.

That dream path led him to Crystal Springs.

The gods at first rejoiced in his escalating madness, until eventually another day came, when a once disconsolate Sying Hao smiled before the elders.

It made them wonder, "What the hell does he have to smile about?"

A Puzzle

Back on the mountain, the two friends woke at first light. Without a fire, and the evening candles long spent, they rose quickly. Both knew a quick burst of activity would ward off the morning chill. Silently they moved in concert, their long wilderness experience evident in their every move. They capped off their water bladders with snow, which would melt as the day warmed. In moments they had packed and already gnawed away at handfuls of sun-dried fish and berries, building energy before heading out.

They instinctively took precautions to knock down the snow shelter and clear all evidence of their stay. They knew not to leave careless traces for anyone tracking their movements. Even here, one could take no chances. The slope now lay renewed with fresh fallen snow. Soon, wind would sweep away whatever tracks they left as they continued their ascent to the higher ridge. By day's end, they crossed over and Bao Ling had his first glimpse of the eastern expanse. It seemed endless. A complex maze of peaks and valleys left by the ages to riddle the minds of encroaching strangers.

Though a different world, Bao Ling already knew where in his field of vision Jing Province lay, just as he knew the straight line to Ling Village. But he said nothing of this to his friend. No sense in plucking an old tune. His heart would always long for home, same as anyone else. Hui knew this, and he waited patiently while his friend stole a moment to look out and to reflect.

Some time after they crossed over, Bao Ling let go the thoughts of home and turned to Hui asking to revisit one of the issues troubling him from the account of the night before.

"One thing continues to puzzle me."

Hui's eyes raised to encourage.

Remembering what was said of the Black Knight, Bao Ling continued, "How is it the Assassin's Mace didn't harm him? Wasn't it touching against his body the whole time? Before he pulled it out to attack Li, you said it was in his sash? How could that be? Was he immune to it in some way?"

Hui reflected, "That's not an easy question to answer. Accounts vary. I only know what I have heard and who's to say if it can be fully trusted. There's quite a bit of history behind it. Shall we start there."

"Go on."

"Well, as I understand, it wasn't always a mace. It started out as a sphere, then became the mace at a later point. From the beginning, the sphere proved quite insidious on its own. Many unexplained disappearances somehow became attributed to the original sphere. More than once, the greatest alchemists in the land received orders from above to unravel its deeper secrets. Ordered, doubtless unwillingly, to enter the sealed inner sanctum where it sat waiting. Usually several together, safety in numbers perhaps. Inexplicably, they seemed simply to have vanished into thin air. The troop outside stood dumbfounded. After allowing ample time for whoever was inside to signal their wish to exit and hearing nothing, the guards became concerned. No one had entered or left, and there were no other exits. Only after entering on their own and investigating did they notice their own footprints traced in what seemed a coating of dust on the clay floor. At first, the significance of this escaped them. It's not even something they would have noticed had they not remembered it had been meticulously clean when last inspected. Since no one came and went, nothing should have changed. The mystery of it frightened them. Then their imaginations took hold. Though suspicions arose, no one at first believed the sphere had the power to disappear people, leaving only ashes and dust in their absence.

"For those in power, what it could do was of course no secret. But explaining it, determining how, and exploiting its propensities to full advantage required careful study. On another recorded occasion, a committee of Shang Dynasty generals, men of the highest rank and skill, received the imperial directive to get to the bottom of the mystery once and for all. More to the point, they were to unravel its strategic implications, and devise uses for it on the battlefield.

"Together they entered. As usual, those outside secured the chamber behind them. Regrettably for the Shang Prince, his trusted commanders became yet another footnote in the string of disappearances. Yet again, ash on the floor. As before, guards peering inside afterwards saw only an empty vault, with the orb seated on its pedestal, unmoving but beckoning to them all like the enchantress Xi Shi[9] spread in ready waiting. *"Could this really be happening?"* they wondered, arguing amongst themselves about what they

---

[9] One of the four beauties of ancient China. So beautiful that when she stared to the pond below her balcony, fish within lost all sense of self and sank helplessly to the bottom.

heard, and what they had imagined. Some suspected trickery or deceit, "We have become their dupes."

"As to the sphere's reputed capacity to steal one's mind, why, they barely had the will to seal the door on leaving. Assuming they all left of course. Back then no one kept count of missing guards, their expendability simply taken for granted. But generals disappearing completely! Unheard of! From that point, anyone with sense avoided all direct contact with the sphere. As for the voices, the incessant beckonings and allures; the promises of bliss, contentment, enlightenment, power or whatever else one sought? The increasing reports, and general consistency among them left little doubt. They were fact! The great minds of the realm surmised, once inside the sealed vault with the sphere, its pleas and inducements became overwhelming, even for the strongest. The will to resist crumbled against what it promised, and what it guaranteed in its world. Who wouldn't leave this life behind? From that point, anyone with any instinct for self-preservation knew not to touch the orb, or to even get close. What it could do was of course no longer secret but exploiting its propensities to full advantage still demanded careful study. Presumably, after trying just about everything at least once; in time, others more clever learned to protect themselves from its unfathomable animus. But even they could not fortify themselves to resist its inexplicable allure. 'How could anyone resist?' they asked, 'always beckoning, forever promising the ever forbidden?' Men, even great warriors, generals, emperors too, none could ignore its call."

"But wait. You said they found a way? What was it? How did they protect themselves?"

"They bagged the sphere."

"They what?"

"Yes, hard to believe, isn't it? Put a hood over it as you approach; secure it; then seal it tightly in a bag."

"Like a snake?"

"Sort of. More like a bird of prey. You've seen hawks trained to hunt? Always ready, always alert and on edge. Their master controls them with a well-placed hood. Cover their eyes and all threats and concerns disappear to them. With the hood in place, they perch almost docile, their wildness there, but momentarily tamed. They'll relax completely, even peck from your hand.

"Likewise, cover the orb, dare not touch it. Any direct contact with its surface promised disappearance, presumably death, or worse. We can only speculate what truly happens to those who have felt its brazen kiss. Though numbering few, there have been eyewitnesses to the disappearances. Some have attested to seeing the spirits of the disappeared ripped involuntarily from their living bodies and sucked helplessly into the darkened pool of its waiting surface. An effect 'like quicksand,' they said. The victim's emptied shell remaining, devoid of life and absent nurturing chi, dropping to the ground, ending as dust, ofttimes not even sparing clothing or armor. The sphere possessed its own mind. It left no trails, no clues; just unsettling mysteries."

"Spirits ripped from living bodies. How can that be? Where do they go? Do they yet live? And the witnesses, can they be relied upon? Would not their own terror cast phantoms where none lay in fact?"

"Now, like them, you understand the scope of the problem, and the price of arriving at understanding. They had the same thoughts as you Bao Ling. The object posed questions which demanded answers, ignored only at considerable risk. True, the eyes may be deceived by the heart and the mind. We know only this; and Master Li can tell you it's true, as can I. When staring deeply into the sphere, one sees the imprisoned spirits of those it has consumed, for a time still visible in their earthly forms; just as they were when taken. Listen intently and you can hear within yourself their calls, their moans, wails, and cries. Looking into its darkness is like glimpsing into the still of a deep night, where there are no stars, only anguished spirits begging for mercy and release."

"And witnesses have said the same?"

"Understandably, most simply turned and ran. A few intrepid sorts refused to believe their senses and pushed forward fearlessly probing for the truth, going directly to the sphere itself and looking closely to see what lay within."

"What did they find?"

"Some lost their sanity. For others, assuming their recollections sound, it would seem those most recently taken clung ever near to the surface where their pleas for release wafted from the movement of their silenced lips."

"Captured and held within? Then perhaps not dead? Surely there is an escape, a remedy, an answer?"

"As to those sorry spirits encased within, none have ever returned or found release. Not even one, and it's been quite a long time. Are they dead? To this world, I would have to say yes. Remember, for most the sphere leaves no traces, ensuring they have nothing to return to. Their once bodies reduced to vapor or dust. Perhaps that explains its meticulousness in eradicating what remains. It would be easier to breathe life into a rock, than to pull a spirit back from that netherworld of lost souls.

"Bao Ling, whatever you do, never forget. With the hood in place, you can hold it and move it. Just be very, very wary."

The Fire Demon Leaves an Egg

Bao Ling thought on this a bit, then spoke the obvious, "That seems almost too easy."

"No, not easy at all—you see, the sphere still calls out to you, its allure all the stronger for its being within its seeming prison. It's as if it were alive, reacting to its confinement. And when it speaks, it speaks to you directly, as if it knew everything about you, your wishes, your needs, and your fears. From there it sends its divine promises of endless contentment cresting upon waves of celestial chimes, doubtless sounded by beckoning virgins, or whatever else it takes to steal attention. Many have learned from sad experience, you can capture the sphere, and you can even hold it; but you can't keep it for long before the allure of its constant whispers grinds your resistance down to where it no longer matters, and you become its willing captive. A temptation which for all but a few has shown itself impossible to bear. Some say even the gods strap tightly to their celestial foundations to resist its will. Could something be so powerful? Gods are gods, we presume immune to things like this. Apart from its curious effect on humans, and the many disappearances which even their divine gazes cannot track or follow, I'm sure they find it more of a curiosity than anything to be concerned about. Surface dwellers disappear, so what? Simply put, just another plague for mankind to contend with. The more the better. It needn't directly concern them."

"Who all did you hear this from? How do you know any of it is true?"

For a moment, Hui's expression clouded with sadness, then he answered, "I've heard this from others, Fa Miu among them, and, as you probably gather, he's no rube. According to the fox[10], the Yellow Knight himself whispered to Li Fung the tricks of sealing the mace, among other things, just as they made their final parting. I've since come to learn for myself, all of it is true."

Bao Ling wondered, *How would he come to know it's true?* That told him more questions remained. But first, he wanted to learn of the mace and its eventual containment.

"What you've said troubles me in one regard."

"How so?" asked Hui.

"Getting back to the original question. When you described Master Li's final challenge, just as he stood against the Black Knight. You said the knight kept the Assassin's Mace secured in his red sash, where all could see its ominous beauty.

"Wasn't the mace touching him the entire time? Why was he not affected by its power?"

"I have no answer for that, beyond rumor. In Wei, they say the Black Knight achieved what no earlier holders of the cursed weapon had been able to. To some notable degree, he had managed to tame it. We know prior to reaching his hands, its effects were unfettered and well appreciated by all in its periphery, who, as a rule, gave it wide berth. Doubtless, it was for that very reason the earliest custodians conjectured the need for the wand, some sort of attachment or device with which to safely convey and utilize to full effect."

---

[10] Referencing Fa Miu, often thought to be sly as a fox.

"Conjectured?"

"Yes, in theory the sphere, powerful though it might be, lacking wieldiness, remained limited in scope of application. Their solution, the wand. This would at least provide some safe distance between the holder and the orb. What appears to us as a mere shaft, transforming the sphere into a mace, culminated a quest spanning over two hundred years for a material adequate to the task. First attempts to mount handles required the sacrifice of countless hapless metal smiths, who became victims themselves. The trials and experiments continued unabated. Alchemists, wizards, and would be assassins searched, studied and tested every conceivable combination of materials and alloys. All unsuccessfully. What could they mount to the sphere as a shaft and brace, securing its reach, yet insulating the holder from its pernicious touch. Succeeding in the hopeless endeavor promised to finally allow its uninhibited use as a battlefield weapon. According to their reckoning, it would assume the geometry and characteristics of the traditional mace. In theory, this would facilitate its safe handling and application. As a weapon, it would have no peer. In the right hands, such a weapon could turn the fates of nations. Best of all, its very existence would remain shrouded. A weapon suspected, but beyond anyone's rational belief.

Still, as always happens in the realm of weapons, with great advances come commiserate risks. Whatever you manage to conjure up, no sooner will you reveal it than its very twin or bastard child will become the bane of your own existence. And that too was the great concern with the mace. You know how it goes. If something exists, what's to say there are not others? What if there were more than one? Who possessed the others? Had those others surpassed the Shang in unraveling its secrets; its potential? You see, powerful as it might be, the greatest fear of those early strategists was that it might fall into the hands of adversaries, or, heaven forbid, already be there. For that very reason, it was fine for others to learn of it, but only as rumor, or battlefield legend, the sightings so rare and uncommon, no one could know or testify for certain whether it existed in fact; or better yet, if there were one or ten thousand of them. "Keep them guessing" became the guiding mantra. Elsewhere, powerful as it might be, it would remain properly hooded and secured, kept in careful reserve only for those moments of precise need, when other, more mundane options could not prevail. Targeted surgically, its effects would work their own magic, timed carefully to capitalize on fear and to engender terror and panic. That explains best why the sphere became godchild to the assassins, finding its own path to Di Xin[11] through Daji—and also, the enduring efforts to devise its wand. Consider for a moment. As a battlefield mace in the hands of one like Guan Yu; one man could turn an entire opposing army to ash."

"Are there no limits to its capacity?"

"None known. If such exist, no one has come close to finding them. Trust me on this, many have tried."

"And the wand?"

"The fruitless research and experimentation continued unabated. After years of endless failure and escalating frustration, legend has it the bone casters and royal prognosticators of Shang predicted a solution to the

---

[11] Di Xin. Last of the Shang emperors and husband to the enchantress Daji. It was Di Xin, at the encouragement of his wife, who made it a life task to perfect the "Assassin's Mace," expecting it to permanently seal his line, and provide a portal to eternal life with his beloved.

conundrum would soon become evident in the heavens. The sphere itself would select its own celestial mate with whom it might forever merge. They foresaw a moonless night, with the skies cloaked in foreboding darkness, blanketing even the stars. Sure enough, the day arrived just as they predicted, and the night sky loomed ominous. The surface world took on the air of a graveyard. From the North, in the region of the Purple Forbidden Enclosure, the heavens glowed red. Reaching from above the horizon, the head of a fire demon emerged, and then its body, at first slowly and full of caution. Once gaining confidence, it ascended upward in the form of a dragon to race across the sky, its incandescent wings tracing a wide arc over the entire field of vision leading like a flaming marker arrow to a final resting place beyond the southern horizon. The soothsayers assured the Shang King Di Xin he would have his assassin's mace if he could find the 'egg' left by the fire demon and then, solve its riddle.

But We're Artists

"Di Xin of Shang? I know little of him."

"Yes. King Di, last of the Shang. Historians have been careful in preserving the record of his debauchery. If only so we might more readily recognize the descent into evil of future leaders, should it ever repeat. Best to slice the legs from beneath them, lest they grow stout and unassailable. So they reasoned. With Di Xin, the devil had already emerged in their midst before anyone even suspected he existed. Among rulers, Di Xin has the dubious distinction of bearing the title *Prince Incarnate of Earthly Evil*."

Bao Ling chuckled at the thought, "Friend Hui, in case you haven't noticed, there's a lot of that going around. I can think of several who we might equally cast as such, or who could give the title a good run for the gold, should they too fall subject to the scrutiny of history."

A stone-faced Hui continued, "Perhaps brother Ling. Then again, your opinion might change if I tell you more of him."

Realizing his friend had chastised him for being just a bit too quick and cavalier, Bao Ling answered deferentially, "Fair enough. What do I need to know."

"They say the great historian Sima Qian chose to live dishonored rather than commit suicide after his unfortunate castration. That's a story for a different day. He rightfully felt only he knew the true lessons from past rulers; and only he could preserve and communicate their record for our later scrutiny and benefit. Through him, we learn of a prince with unmatched talent who suddenly departs from righteousness and morality, abandons all responsibilities, and surrenders to darkness. It made no sense, then or now, and all were at a loss trying to explain or understand. Some say he had been bespelled by his wicked wife Daji. Many deem her to have been a witch; or a soul possessed."

"Possessed? The sphere. Do you suppose?"

"Yes, I do suppose; but in what specific way, I cannot say. I'll share what I know and what others have said, perhaps you will have a better take on this than I.

"The accounts of their evil union ring so horrific, even speaking of them makes one feel tainted. Among their favored proclivities, a penchant for heating a bronze cannon to glowing red, then lining prisoners up for a final not too subtly nuanced sexual escapade, ordering they mount and embrace the glowing stem, admiring in sublime ecstasy as the victims descended the sputtering slope into agony and excruciating death. By then, the horror surrounding them had become so perverse and pervasive, no one could glean the courage to resist or even object. Punishment in the first, second or third degree was one thing, but these two had mastered the bizarre and the obscene, and their irrefutable genius in cultivating prolonged and excruciating pain anchored their reputation for terror.

"In the end, only one person, the righteous minister Bi Gan dared to speak. Bi Gan had proven his worth to the empire over a lifetime of constant service. As uncle and one time protector to Di Xin, his past counsel was highly valued and deemed sagely—even when critical of the King's nascent disturbing leanings. Given their past, his reprimands were ofttimes tolerated. But like the scoldings of a worried parent, in the end disregarded. All that of course before the great descent, and the corresponding emergence to power of his wife-instigator, Daji. For that very reason, Queen Daji feared the old man above all others, and like a wild fox would cower and snarl whenever the minister neared the imperial chamber. All knew the day would come when the goodly Bi Gan could bear her presence no more and would have to abandon all cautions and reservations to speak his own true mind. He had weighed the prospects and the alternatives, as well as the anticipated consequences, and in the end deemed only he had the weight of relationship to speak truth to his nephew, and to perhaps penetrate the evil cocoon which had now fully enveloped him."

"Be careful Bi Gan. Evil doesn't like hearing about itself."

"How true, Brother Ling. Imagine for a moment how Di Xin listened in silent awe as his uncle detailed the record of atrocities and made certain his nephew fully understood how precarious his own position had become among his ministers, his generals, and most importantly, the people. The great preponderance of his subjects now buckled to their knees from the incessant demands for indentured labor and increasing taxes; all while the King created lakes of wine and islands of meat laden trees for his perverse enjoyment of a twisted alternate to reality; creating a new dimension onto himself and his possessed-by-evil wife."

"But we're artists," the nephew protested. "You mistake our unique talents for abandonment of responsibility, even referring to them as debauchery. Tell me uncle, where is the fairness in that? We lead by example. How will the peasants ever find any joy being mere peasants? It's for us to show them the way out. A clear and unmistakable method to release themselves from all the inhibitions and constraints which imprison their very souls. Just like that (snapping his fingers)! One moment you're in, tied up in knots: the next you're out! Daji and I are free spirits, the only truly free spirits in the land. It's not easy you know. Try to understand and show some sympathy, or perhaps appreciation. We work at it constantly; why, in case you haven't noticed, we hardly ever sleep. This isn't easy. Would you have us become like them? Is it not better to show them the possibilities once they shed their subservient skins? Should they not aspire to be all they can be?"

"The boy remains quick as ever," thought Bi Gan. He scolded his nephew in his precisely measured riposte. "There (pointing to a nearby wall opening) sits your suffering kingdom, and your impoverished people. There (now pointing to the Queen) sits the embodiment of evil. Everyone whispers she has stolen your once noble soul. You (pointing finally to Di Xin) are the scion of heaven, ordained to stand forever between the two, and to protect the victim from the scourge. Do not fail in your sacred duty! Do not abandon your people (his voice raised to a thunderous scream, to the abject horror of all present)!"

Though still quick and clever, King Di Xin knew he would not prevail by bantering further with his clever and now outraged old uncle.

Only then did Daji come mouselike (and ever cautiously) forward. She offered, "I may have a solution. The matter simply requires a more penetrating analysis." She walked alongside her husband, and from the rear, whispered delicately into his right ear.

Bi Gan saw only her serpent's tongue pushing deep into the ruler's ear canal, seeming to extend its reach far within, as though penetrating to the very center of his nephew's skull.

For a moment, he looked about, wondering if others saw the same. Clearly, if they did, their expressions gave no hint.

The King smiled as though lost in ecstasy, "Yes, a carefully executed study will surely enlighten us."

King Di Proclaims
Uncle Bi a Sage

He then thanked his uncle profusely, both for his candor and his exemplary courage, even forgiving the momentary lapse of protocol and the raised voice, saying how it brought back fine memories of his youth. Looking scornfully about to the sycophants ever present among his retinue he added, "We should all be so inclined to candor." Driving the point home, he concluded the session with a formal proclamation to his scribes acknowledging Bi Gan as sage of the realm. With notable pomp and formal ceremony, he graciously dismissed Bi Gan, politely taking his uncle's arm and guiding him to the exit.

Bi Gan turned about just before leaving, looking long at his nephew, his anguished expression now weighted in despair.

Di Xin returned the gaze, for a moment, seeming almost uncertain where he stood, a crease in his brow as his thoughts raced fruitlessly about. Perhaps looking to flush out recollections of life moments shared, long since purged. Daji tactfully placed herself between the two, beatifically smiling toward her husband.

"Ah, there you are. Thank you, my wife, for returning me to my senses. You remind I have become a new man, a beacon for the age. I must remember this. Uncle remains stuck and mired in his ill-considered concerns and reservations. A prisoner no different

from the peasants. Not a bit of artist in him at all. It falls to me to release him from his bondage. We'll all be the better for it."

The other counselors, seeing how Bi Gan's conviction did in fact bring formal honor and recognition, now cursed themselves for missing what had proven in hindsight to be an opportunity to achieve distinction, no easy feat in this troubled court.

Their jealousy ended abruptly; and very soon thereafter.

You see, even hindsight has a hindsight.

With a flick of his forefinger, Di Xin beckoned his ever-present chief of security.

"Sir!" the Captain called, coming forward before his leader in anticipation of a command.

"Bring me his heart!"

Stunned, the warrior hesitated, "Begging your patience sir, I'm not sure I understand."

Instantly, Di Xin reached for the soldier's sheathed dagger, and before the stunned sentry could think to react, had pulled it loose and affixed its pointed tip to the owner's chest. Then, nudging its razor talon slowly forward, he began to draw blood. "I want you to take this blade, and this point, and drive it carefully into Bi Gan's chest, being certain to miss the heart. Then, just as carefully carve an opening with this fine razor edge you have so meticulously honed. Through that same opening, reach in, take out the beating heart; slice it free it from its confine, and deliver it to me immediately for close study and analysis.

Horrified, the guard felt *"This offends all reason and crosses all lines of propriety for a professional officer."*

"Sir, why not just kill him where he stands?"

"Don't be a fool, Captain. How will we ever completely know the heart of a learned sage, if we don't seize the opportunity? We must study it carefully and precisely when the privilege is present before our very eyes. In this barren land, how many sages do you think there are? He's it! If you know of others, bring them to me. If not, shut your mouth before I have your tongue removed and boiled for you to swallow whole. Quick! Bring me his beating heart. Chop Chop! Move out!"

No sooner had he finished than the eager Daji ran to the security chief. Projecting shame and embarrassment, she apologized profusely for her husband's impetuous nature. Then, unable to turn her attention from the scarlet drip trickling slowly from the sentry's tunic, lifted the garment with the words "Here, let me check." Then to the shock and utter dismay of all present (but for her husband) began to zealously lick the wound clean. Instantly, yet inexplicably, the guard sensed his erection pushing hard and forward as the King yielded his knowing smile, nodding with upturned eyes in resignation and in complete understanding of the guard's predicament. *"She's got you now lad. Careful. Before you know it, she'll be mounting you and riding her new little pony naked while carted through the imperial halls."*

"I would do anything to have this woman," thought the Captain, feeling her hands now working everything they could find beneath his tunic. Whatever reservations he had fell silent. Why, he couldn't even recall what they were.

Daji stepped back, smiling broadly, making careful eye contact with the now liquified officer as her tongue danced like a lure before him, rolling carefully over her lips, taking in whatever traces of red lingered, finishing afterward by licking her fingers clean, one at a time.

The Captain turned to Di Xin and extended his hands, "My weapon sir. I'll need it for the job."

"Of course you will. Make haste young man." Di Xin smiled as he carefully passed the weapon, handle first, to the sentry.

For a fleeting instant, just as the etched bone handle returned to his grip, the Captain felt the eruption of a countering urge. The knife had its own thoughts on the matter. "Kill them!" it pleaded, "Now! While they stand before you! You alone can end the misery. Save us! Save yourself!"

"Shit!" thought the guard, "Now the knife speaks to me. This is too spooky! What the hell next? Will I awaken and find this all to be a dream and myself lost in the land of spirits?"

He hesitated just a bit, looking at the King and then his wife. They too had heard the calling from the blade. In their altered universe, the living essence of all things had become clear to their awareness, as did its many forms and voices. They knew full well; a cloud, a rock, a beast, even a blade might have its own thoughts and reservations when ordered to act at odds with its inherent disposition. Dispositions? Wouldn't you know it? They resided everywhere. Did not everything have a Buddha nature?

The blade had upheld the disposition instilled by its caring maker. It had even spelled out for its holder's benefit what to do.

All to no avail.

The regal pair smiled warmly at the Captain, already presaging the blade's objections would come to naught. In the court of weakness and appetite, they ruled supreme, crushing all resistance using their feathers of persuasion touching upon hopeless points of longing. The shrewd Daji had her counter set to play, even in fact before she first entered the room. For the Captain, these were uncharted waters. Daji had long before done her ten thousand repetitions, perfecting every subtlety and nuance of what it took to make a man lose himself in her vast realm of desires promised and ofttimes granted.

Surprised she would grant them? Where would her credibility lie if they weren't? Her reputation had taken firm root. Besides, she truly craved the play. She confidently stepped before the Captain, set her lavendered hands delicately upon his upper arms, showing no concern or fear over the tip of the knife now touching lightly upon her left breast, she seemed even to enjoy it, stalling just a bit to savor its pressing to her nipple, yet still unable to push forward on its own, frozen tightly in the battle tested officer's trembling hand. Regarding it no further, she stood high on her toes, then lightly tugged him toward her lips where she whispered into his ear, tongue slicing delicately through the folds. "Do this for me my love, and before the sun sets, I will have you kneeling entwined before my hidden jewel."

"Such very strange times," thought the Captain, *"Here we idle about in hell, presumably waiting for Yama to take charge, but he never does. Where can he be? Seeing him now would be a welcome relief, laying the need for all further speculation to rest. Except for this one possibility. I fear I have split from existence."*

With his despairing heart ever more certain, the officer knew then what he must do. A done deal. This would be his ticket out. Once done, boundless bliss would be his reward. All for the price of a mere beating heart taken from a spent old fool. Long years of sacrifice and stalled ambition now yielded their untold dividends.

How easily one's judgment becomes twisted and bent by suppressed needs, hidden wants, and the promise of desires soon fulfilled.

Sheathing his blade, he made a quick exit, hoping to run down Bi Gan while still within the imperial halls.

Shi-Hi Ke stopped his narration at that point, electing to pause on the slope, as though surveying their continuing route. Or struggling with what to say next?

As they again continued, he remained silent, until Bao Ling, now fully invested in the outcome, could hold his patience no longer. He pleaded for Hui to continue.

Never Surrender

"Di Xin, like many wicked men, exhibited immense potential for good until the day he turned. Historian Sima Qian takes great care to tell us how, in the early years, Di Xin showed remarkable promise as a ruler. He wants all to know the vulnerability of good and righteousness against the insidious lure of temptation.

"The scope of Di's intellect inspired awe, few could hold argument with him and expect to win. He stood steadily with truth, and his keen perception usually anchored him tightly to that place, even when others drifted elsewhere under the influence of time and uncertainty. His diverse talents extended virtually everywhere and included music, art, astrology, as well as Jiao Li, the already ancient grappling art. He handpicked his personal bodyguards from the most skilled proponents in the land, and he regularly scoured the competitions looking for additions to his stable.

"It became the fate of this particular warrior clan, under the influence of his careful nurturing, and in the end his deviant hand, to devolve into the supreme assassin's confrerie. In another time, they came under the guidance of the Black Knight, whose acquaintance you may already have made. To a man, the brotherhood referred to King Di as Shifu. They recognized and honored his great skills, and his patriarchal guidance in establishing their crucial role within the hidden bowels of the realm. As a master of the martial sciences, he towered above all. Surpassing even the best from his legion of assassins. Why, when he hunted, we hear he preferred to go alone into the wilderness, without an escort, bearing no weapons. The court marveled how he rarely failed to bag his prey, be it a rabbit, a deer, a bear or panther. Through ceaseless dedication and endless practice and application, he showed to have mastered several of the ancient esoteric styles. Once thought lost and extinct, they survived through him, bequeathed in time through his sinister legacy. Even today, their ripples continue, now spread world-wide like a rampant plague.

"Mirroring the arts of the common people, they included the internal and the external, the hard and the soft. But in the core, they differed. They served utility, and catered to the elite, inevitably veering from righteousness. One almost thinks of the noble Liu Bei when gauging Di Xin's potential. In some ways, the young king even surpassed the noble Liu. Regretfully, as sometimes happens, a talent with no seeming limit suddenly deviates from its potential and like a missile turned abruptly by unseen winds, angles inexplicably downward, and away from the heavens it once sought."

Bao Ling thought of his own mentor when he heard of Di Xin's martial prowess. True, he had encountered many teachers, but only one brought sense and purpose to the whole lifetime mix. But for Sying Hao, Bao Ling would be living like a hunted beast. Surviving and running, ever anticipating his own death, or the next kill. He suspected Sying Hao could match Di Xin's skills in many respects, even exceed them in some. But then, unexpectedly, within his thoughts a crooked thread arose. He would never have considered this before hearing the account of Di Xin. *"If one such as Di Xin might be corrupted, what does that say for Sying Hao?"*

He shuddered at the prospect. True, they had become like brothers, yet in many ways, Bao Ling still regarded Sying Hao as the elder, his own Shifu. *"What if he faltered? How would I know? What would that mean for me? Who could stand in the way of someone like that? Besides me?"*

"Poisonous thoughts" he whispered to himself. So far removed, yet even in that very moment, the lingering resonance of Di Xin's legacy might still unsettle the minds of the strong, and the noble.

Bao Ling could barely cloak the panic on his face as he looked up to Shi-Hui Ke, "How precarious we humans can be. Just when you're sure you know someone, and expect them to be just as you reckon, your impression lifts like a mist as harsh reality tears into your once clarity."

Hui studied and weighed the concern evident in Bao Ling's words. As though reading his thoughts, he replied, "How true. Yet we have no choice but to wean through the chaff to find the grain. No one can go it alone (looking hard at Bao Ling, even pausing for effect), and expect to survive whole. The weight of responsibility is too great. Sima Qian took especial care to show us not all men succumbed to the imperceptible flaws of character which unlocked the cages of evil hidden within Di Xin. What happened with Di Xin may well have drawn the attention of the sages who followed. Buddha tells us those propensities persist within all of us, whether real or illusory; and it is for us through vigilance, discipline and fearlessness to gather the reins and push through, freeing ourselves into reality and awareness. Therein lies lasting freedom. The hedonistic chartings of Di Xin and Daji promise freedom but instead bind one forever in vacuous self-affirmation. Recognizing the same, the master Kongzi[12] created his supreme architecture of behavior and social order predicated on ren[13], compassion, self-discipline, and restraint, leaving no doubt he too appreciated the problem within, and sought to show us how to live without its hijacking our essential virtues."

"And Laozi[14]?" asked Bao Ling.

"Laozi of course said nothing directly. Indirectly, he said plenty. In the sage's classic Dao De Jing, one can sense a complete rejection of all things exemplified by Di Xin and Daji, and others like them."

Bao Ling recalled the many scrolls, and Sying Hao's ceaseless study and self-questioning, never relenting for a moment. Now he began to see the reason. To that very end, his friend had chosen seclusion over influence at court. He might have chosen to go elsewhere, anywhere, and ended up at the top. Other rulers would have made him their general, or their trusted son-in-law. He could have risen high in any court. But his loyalties lay with Shu, where Colonel Sun had first cast his lot with Zhuge Liang. He often made it a point to carefully remind the younger Bao Ling, "Always do the work little brother. Life can be like a sea full of storms, though it has its occasional fine moments of beauty and beguiling wonder. The work you do in preparation will be your vessel. It will carry you through the storms and ensure you remain true to yourself. Just as the pine keeps its green in winter, wisdom perseveres in and through hardship. Accept those challenges. Never

---

[12] Confucius (551–479 BCE)

[13] Humanity. As in the sense of striving to push up all others and improving their lot.

[14] Laozi - (604 - 532 BCE). One of history's great sages. Said to have authored the "Dao de Ching."

surrender!"

Treachery at Court Turns Di Xin

"As I'm sure you've already begun to suspect, it came to pass only Di Xin and his wife Daji controlled the evil sphere. He appears to have come upon her and the orb together, or rather, they came upon him. Raised from birth to be an assassin, born into one of the prominent sanctioning clans, with her great skills and unmatched beauty, she propelled herself to the very apex of the clandestine order. There, through a process of trick, device, deceit and carefully rationed pleasure, she soon became handmaid to the orb, now her "hidden jewel."

As she confided to Di Xin, one lucky day, within her secretive enclave, the chieftain blessed her with the supreme task. Assassinate the King. In this instance, the still annoyingly righteous Di Xin. *"You will remove him from existence,"* read the order. She knew exactly what that meant, and why she was the one chosen. She knew how to go about it, but she also knew better. Many were sure to profit and garnish influence with him gone, and no price to achieve that end stood too steep. Heavens, what their self-serving foolishness was about to unleash! Had they only known beforehand. Regretfully, such is the blindness of unbridled greed and the lust for power. Without great caution and attention to consequences or unanticipated outcomes, such faults will take no one anywhere soon.

"In him, with him, and through him, she envisioned the actualization of her own potential. Finally, a mate who could match the breadth and scope of her intellect, ambition, and as it turned out, her own multifarious desires. Until then, all subsumed by her harsh assassin's role, which she would now relinquish like the useless old skin of a maturing snake. As Queen and soul mate to Di Xin she secured the freedom to release the unbounded stream of her long sublimated and repressed inclinations. Nothing would ever again stand in her way. She confessed all. King Di learned of the plot, and its inception within the very heart of his own court. Funded by the most prominent families and endorsed even by his closest ministers and trusted counselors. This knowledge left him devastated. Who wouldn't have been? Daji showed him the irrefutable proof. There could be no doubt or argument to the contrary. She needed no trickery or deception here. Even those accused could not deny their complicity. The evidence overwhelmed."

"How could my righteous conduct and example lead to this end?" he agonized.

Having no ready answer, and unable to bear the thought of it repeating, he might well have chosen to end his own life. You see, for him, the world had turned inside out. Imagine a forest where roots pointed to the heavens, and leaves grew within the earth. The universe you thought you ruled supreme lay elsewhere, and beyond your reach. Topsy, turvy, all had become perverse. And he, set forever adrift. Inexplicably, and unbearably isolated.

Adrift that is, but for the guiding hand of Daji, who had already anticipated his troubled heart and would have ready the answers he called for.

"When righteous conduct leads to disaster, it must find new bearings."

"I don't understand."

Then, she revealed her hidden jewel. Taking the orb from its cover, she set it carefully before him.

Instinctively, he reached for it, she stopping him just in time. "Careful, this was to be the means for your assassination."

"What are you saying? A black orb? Some sort of decorative stone? Yet somehow a weapon?"

She smiled glowingly, almost childlike in her eagerness to share a lifetime of secrets and repressed desires with her soon-to-be soul mate.

And that she did. For the next several hours, she revealed all, punctuated by wild orgiastic intermissions where she carefully brought home each point. His intellect dove into the significance of this great gift she had delivered at his moment of dire need.

The isolation lifted. Until that moment, Di Xin had lived an austere existence, almost ascetic, forged by self-denial, driven toward perfection of character. That ended.

In one cathartic session, Daji proved to him the absurdity of it all. From this point, only pleasure and complete gratification of desire would prove true in their self-forged reality. Reality because you felt it to the core, nothing matched the power and intimacy of its touch. No other roots to perception stood so convincing. Others might have their games, and their machinations. These two would be free from all of it. Heaven had sealed its approval, countenancing the unlikely sequence of events making her Queen to his King, and unwittingly delivering to them the power of the orb.

In their fathomless joy, even still entwined, they marveled at the face of the orb all the while entranced by its mysteries. Before them spun the world of anguished spirits seeking release from within, their faces streaming and floating endlessly beneath its glistening surface.

"Beautiful, isn't it? Like clouds. I could watch them all day."

"And what of righteousness?" he asked.

"Ah my love, that is the perfection of it. From this point, you define righteousness, and I pronounce you free to let it take whatever form you wish. A new order. With the orb, all will learn to follow your lead, and I will be at your side, intimate in every way, and eager to serve and inspire."

By then, his resistance had thinned. Even when her lips no longer moved, he heard her voice of promise and allure everywhere about him. At first, he thought the unpent intensity of newfound ecstasy had driven him from his senses. He wasn't sure what he was seeing or hearing. He looked to Daji, she stood still and silent, like a goddess, returning his gaze and peering into his soul. The heat from her stare burned through whatever restraint or caution remained. His own eyes fired back, proclaiming without doubt his singularity among men, and his now ignited passion for Daji. Then, as though responding to its call, they both turned to the orb. He knew now. She had come to him bearing utter clarity, and with her blade of intimacy had excised all restraint and self-denial from his being.

They had been like weights on his soul. Not virtues, but rather impediments to his release from the weight of the mundane which is now what he saw his prior life to be. Only then did he first hear the sweet callings of its silken voice. At first, he confused it with the luscious whispers of Daji, still resonating within. The delicate inflections so similar. Daji's sibilant murmurs were there one moment, then subsumed within the turn of a greater wave. A rumble now amplified to where what had only sounded a moment before, now coursed his arteries, titillating every nerve and point on his body. The orb promised all, and through the two of them, would make all possible. With the globe as their lodestar, they became as a trinity, in their thinking and their complicity in the fulfillment of its destiny. All other responsibilities paled to insignificance.

In that very instant, he veered inexplicably downward. Away from the realms of righteousness to which all men must aspire, or in the end become lost.

Hui continued, "Evil comes in many flavors. Do you suppose their brand of evil resonated so well to its palate, the orb beckoned its own tail from the heavens in the form of a fiery tongue seeking completion thru them?"

"Thus accounting for the appearance of the Fire Demon, and the foretelling of its egg in the south. Doubtless, afterward, he spared no effort to find it."

Hui affirmed, "Which of course he soon enough did. Does it surprise that it proved to be a substance unlike any previously known? Stone, metal, jade, wood, flesh? The scholars puzzled and argued, all to no avail. A riddle stumping even the alchemists, one of whom was over five hundred years old. If anyone had seen everything, he surely had. The object possessed the properties of all elements, and at the same time, none of them. It could be everything, and anything, or nothing whatsoever. There it lay before them, impervious. It resisted heat as well as cold and repelled the blows of the heaviest mallets and mauls brought to shape it."

Di Xin Rescues the Egg

"Yet another mystery?" asked Bao Ling.

"Yes, but one which resolved itself. Turned out they found a method to shape it. To do so required constant abrasion, over an inordinately long span of time."

"How in the world did they come up with that?"

"A serendipitous discovery. Of course they had tested for susceptibility to abrasion early on, usually engaging subtle attempts so as not to harm the egg unintentionally. To that end the craftsmen of the realm strained their wits to progress quickly as possible. The impatient King, more so his wife, always inclined to make evident their displeasure. That usually meant designating random tradesmen to the task of refining the efficacy of their techniques on the downslope of the glowing red cannon. Some returned with arms burned completely off, most simply embraced the cannon, preferring quick death to the alternative. For the royal couple, the perverse pleasure gleaned gave temporary respite from the incessant delays as trials of river sand, shark skin, crushed shell, flint, and lava proved completely useless in shaping the egg.

"But for leaving a fine surface sheen, these efforts yielded nothing whatsoever. Nor did anything else seem to have any effect. During the run of sleepless nights and endless tests and trials, one of the many distressed workers, doubtless pushed beyond the constraints of his own wits, somehow got hold of a stone ceremonial ax from an imperial guard room. Then he began pounding on the egg's textured surface like a man possessed.

By what? You can guess as well as I. Did he count on its ceremonial nature, or its antiquity to give it a one up over the ordinary mallets, which had already shown no effect? At first, no one approached to stop him. Then when others came drawn by the berserker run amok, rather than restrain him, they elected to humor his frenzy. Some even encouraged him, figuring no harm would come from it. He even knocked it from its pedestal mount, chasing and striking wildly after it as it rolled about the floor. Like a dog snapping after a rabbit. Quickly enough, this became a game. He would set it on the pedestal, take a mighty swing, then as it flew away, chase after it, cursing and swinging wildly about. Eventually, he would tire and recover his wind, replacing it to the pedestal, pause for rest, then do it all over again. Hell, why should they stop him? They all felt the same as he! At some level, they too wanted to destroy the damn thing; or at least punish the uncooperative egg, split open its shell, somehow force it to yield its heart, yet having no inkling or suspicion as to what purpose or ultimate end.

"Only Di Xin and Daji knew the full purpose. Oh, and most certainly so too did the orb.

"Well, next morning the King walked his usual rounds, which typically first included a check on what developed overnight. Each day, he awoke hopeful, expecting progress with unlocking its mysteries. On this day, after tossing and turning through a mostly sleepless night, he found himself suddenly startled and wide awake. Something had disturbed him, called to him, for he rose much earlier than usual.

Those in attendance would have subdued the berserker well in advance had they known his excellency would be coming, but they didn't. So, to their utter dismay (and surely you can understand why), their sleep-deprived eyes lifted in horror as Di Xin entered their makeshift compound far sooner than expected. There he found not carefully monitored or supervised experimentation, but rather a madman running amok like a rooster in search of a fallen head hellbent on catching and destroying the dragon's egg.

"The loon could not explain himself when confronted by the King. He found himself tongue tied in wonderment over the stone ax, still gripped tightly in his hand, pleading with him to strike at the King's head, now within easy reach. It certainly promised to be a much softer target to crack. *"Get him now, while you can!"* Dumbfounded, the man hesitated, then looked about, wondering if anyone else had heard the command issuing from the heart of the ax. The very same ax had only an instant before commanded he destroy the egg, and at this, though he tried valiantly he failed miserably. Moments were indeed rare when the King did not have his personal guard, as was the case this early morning. Had the guard been in attendance, they would have dispatched the ax wielder instantly. Insubordination was a capital offense. They had the King's standing order to act upon these things as they saw fit.

"Di Xin was glad they weren't there. As he had done many times with beasts in the wild, he put this once human, now turned wild man, under his dulling spell. Not missing a beat, Di Xin extended his hands saying, 'Give it here now, I want to try.'

"Slowly the lunatic raised the ax, then after giving due consideration, decided it best not to go for the soft target. His own survival understandably now pointedly at stake, he calculated best to play it safe, go with the current. Of course, you and I know well, the time to strike is when the opportunity presents. For him, in his delirium, the opportunities and the timings had somehow disjoined. So, opting for caution, and hoping for the best, he turned the ax slowly about and passed it handle-first into Di Xin's waiting hands. The King scrutinized the relic, one of many placed strategically within the palace walls, where they had become a relied weapon and instrument, oft favored by his personal guard for their 'special tasks and assignments.' How easily something first fashioned to serve the sacred, could turn to the profane. These weapons were ageless, made from ganyu[15], a transparent mineral typically colored or shaded, depending on its source or the impurities within, the red and blue variants much esteemed as gemstones. The mundane specimens became axes. Deemed harder than jade, the mineral would polish to a mirror sheen, and sharpen to a precise edge. The secrets of doing this were well established long before the Shang. A technology becoming extinct, even then, though preserved in these specimens which were integral to the imperial armory, and to the many sacrificial ceremonies hoping to influence the will of the heavens in the affairs of men. They had become quite the favorite among Di Xin's select assassins. They relished the unmistakable resonance when the weapon impacted its unfortunate targets. So much for ceremony. King Di looked to the madman, then to the ax, seeing that despite its hardness, fresh cracks, chips and fissures had resulted from his unbridled and relentless assault on the egg. *"That's one fucking hard egg to crack."* passed through his mind. He

---

[15] Corundum

thought to summon the guard, but then hesitated, *"Why let this opportunity for a little fun pass me by?"*

So, this particular affair, the King elected to handle for himself, his once supreme martial skills no less formidable for his seeming indolence. *"These folks lack motivation; their frustrations are obviously grinding them down. They should have come talk to me; I understand things like that. It's well I surprised them this day. Keeps them on their toes. Now that we've identified the problem, I'll teach them how to solve it. Always set proper example, that's the sure way to get things done!"* The sound of a loud whack filled the room, and the once lunatic axeman stood headless for a brief moment while the self-proclaimed artist-King admired the fast-erupting geyser of red spray showering onto the tiled floor. Ironic indeed, the torso frozen headless in time had no further inclination to race about like a rooster.

"Aaahhh" thought King Di, now in the role of resident artist, studying from all perspectives the pattern emerging on the floor *"Looks like a phoenix in flight, a very auspicious sign."*

"Only when assured his improvisational masterpiece had run to its full completion did he return his attention to the egg. *'I'd better check it'* he thought, *'make sure the imbecile didn't render it useless! First things first though.'*

"He ordered his attendants bring a silk panel to the chamber, then had them press it against the tile bound red phoenix, thinking to lift the still moist image and preserve it for Daji's enjoyment. He took care to scribe his royal moniker and the verse, 'Ripened fruit falls to earth when touched by a fickle hand. Look there! Out of the pooling red richness, a phoenix springs forth from emptiness!'

"Not for a moment foregoing his concern, he went next to the egg, studying it closely even as he approached. On first nearing, he found nothing amiss. From an arm's length, all looked as it should. Still, he felt compelled to scan it closely, scouring every cun[16]. To that purpose he stepped directly to the egg, at first walking about, scrutinizing every spot and aspect on its exposed surface. He had long ago committed all of this to his near perfect memory. Then, as he had many times in the past, he caressed it then lifted it from its cradle as though it were a beloved infant, and warmed it in his arms, all the while studying its texture carefully, seemingly neither flesh nor mineral, almost leatherlike in nature, though petrified to the touch. He spoke to it as though it could hear, mindful of the sphere, which definitely could, promising the two would soon become one, united forever as the star gazers had foretold. Only he knew the full thread of the prophecy, and what to do, but first he must unravel the mystery of the egg. In its present form, there could be no union with the sphere. *"We've got to free your heart"* It fell to him to bring them together. *"Even if it ultimately means the loss of my empire, the two of you will be melded into one!"*

---

[16] Chinese inch … ten cun equals one chi.

Whims of a Raging Lunatic

The other members of the research group, scholars from all specialties, alchemists, as well as artisans and smiths of the highest caliber kept their careful distance staring on in utter horror, gluing themselves along the outer walls, not one of them wanting to draw any undue attention upon himself. The consequences of such folly lay all too evident in the grisly scene playing before them. Until that day, the berserker had been a regular chap, a bit strange of course, but just like any of them, looking only to survive another threat-sown day in this hapless asylum. To a person, they remorsed his loss. *"Will I be next?"* their collective mantra.

Suddenly the King called out, "What the hell? What's this? A scratch. Right on the surface. Come here and look at this you fools!"

Of course, not one of them was so foolish as to be the first to voluntarily come forward.

"Guards!" screamed the usually unnervingly calm Di Xin, "Guards!" he called again, only louder.

A squad of sentries poured into the chamber.

"When I clap my hands, execute whoever remains cowering along the perimeter!"

Instantly their cross bows were in hand, arrows placed, and fingers set on bronze triggers. All bows lifted, aimed and readied.

As he pulled his hands apart and threatened to clap, the group moved as one toward the room's center, where the oblong egg sat returned to its pedestal.

"Ah, the impact of the visual. Why waste words promising threats when the mere immediacy of it, even in bluff, pounds like a hammer."

"You," pointing to one of them, "Come here!"

One of the more ancient alchemists glided forward.

With five hundred years under his gown, he knew evil when it stood before him. This King wore its very crown. Though barely more than an astral vapor, undetectable to the normal senses, the stench of death emanated like a sour protoplasm from every bodily orifice of the royal personage, nearly downing the old sage.

As to the dragon's egg, just beyond the King, he felt nothing, though he stretched his finely tuned awareness far forward to its very surface. Neither good nor bad, inert, or dormant. But in the background atmosphere of the room, of the halls, and of the palace itself, if he listened carefully, his time-tuned ears heard the incessant wailing pitch of the orb, constantly pining for its completion. No different than any brazen child screaming its unrelenting wants. Could it be so innocent? He had never seen the orb, nor had anyone spoken of its existence. He simply knew it existed by its wail and its pleading—and from that, innocence be damned, he knew to fear it and what it might do.

You'd think someone old as he would have gotten past fear. He used to think so too.

Everything about this place terrified him. In his once seclusion, he had already achieved the highest mystical states. Levitation, invisibility, near immortality, even some of the ever-elusive transformations. Through dedication, discipline and hard careful work, he pushed through every earthly obstacle. On occasion, he had found, then departed for emptiness and returned. Somehow skirting even his own death, though recently, not always quite by choice. Out to the very heart of the dustless void, where he would have chosen to remain if he could have only shaken the 'voice within' who felt to be making the choice. Ahhh, the interminable voice within. You know who that is. We all hear it. Distractions, distractions, distractions. Always beckoning, always distracting. First this, then that. A leaden anchor centered in the sea of infinite illusion. That's how he viewed what we think to be our selves. Do you think he was right? Who do you think is asking?

"Uncle!" the King addressed the sage deferentially, "Come close. Study the surface with your knowing eye. Confirm for me what I see."

"What is it that you see, Sire?" inquired the sage.

"God damn it you fool! How can you confirm for me what I see, if I already tell you what it is before you see it for yourself? Look at the damn thing! We are all seekers of truth and reality, are we not? You know the rules of proof as well as I. Study it closely. Find what you can, then state it for all as though your life depended on it. Then I will let you know if you confirmed or didn't confirm what I saw! And don't worry about failure. If we can't get corroboration from you, I'm content to let others try."

Hearing those words, the sage sensed his life quest would soon conclude. Standing there, he reflected on the years, centuries in fact, of diligence, work, study, and sometimes, seclusion and meditation; all unknowingly leading to and culminating in this very moment standing here, subject to the whims of a raving lunatic. *"You would think I deserved better than this. Certainly, my karma can't be all that bad."*

Had he done anything different in all that time, he would likely have ended elsewhere. Spared this glimpse into a reality so harsh even his once belief all was but an illusion had now too proven to be an even more encompassing illusion. *"Finding comfort in knowing all to be an illusion has proven unmistakably to be an even more challenging illusion."* This new understanding, enlightenment if you will, came at no easy price. That at least, he saw all too clearly. The glimmer of a smile lit across his lips. *"Perhaps true awareness comes wrapped in layers of illusory sacrifices."*

He had no regrets. It had still been a grand, arduous, yet joyful experience. In retrospect, can we expect more? This unanticipated end turn would count to be little more than a ripple when measured against all the rest, no matter what the outcome.

He turned to the pedestal, then moved closer to study the egg.

He's in remarkable condition for an ancient observed the King. *Might there be a way for Daji and myself to attain such longevity? Is it possible a stew from his remains could achieve that end? You are what you eat, you know. I must ask his thoughts on this when we're finished here. Of course, I'll have to check what he says with the other ancients. With these guys, nothing's ever simple, they're always holding something back. They think they're so clever. I'll just talk them up a bit. There's no better way to flush out the truth than to compare the clumsy efforts of others rashly hoping to deceive you in the moment.*

At first, he saw nothing. For a moment, he wondered if he was being set up for the fall. Reduced to a mere playful foil on the way to re-birthing as a phoenix or dragon on some clay tile floor. Admonishing himself to keep focused, he looked even more closely to the egg, all the while struggling to clear his mind from further distractions.

"May I lift it from the pedestal sire?"

"Of course not. You're not the King. I am. No kingee, no liftee!"

Di Xin looked around to see if his attempt at humor drew any reactions. All faces turned to stone, waiting for his lead before signaling concurrence.

"Sire, with all due respect, I must examine all of the egg before I can deliver a conclusion you can rely on."

Di Xin whispered, "Oh all right, pick the god-damned thing up and do what you must do. Hold on for a moment!" Raising his voice, he turned to the group "Everyone in the room close your eyes until I tell you to open them" then back to the sage, "There, what no one sees, no one will know. You can tell them I picked it up and held it for you."

"Why don't we do that sire? You hold, while I inspect."

"Hey, who's giving the orders here? Who's working for who? Are you trying to belittle me in front of my subjects?"

He lifted the stone ax, making clear the gravity of his point. Before it sliced, the old sage frantically interjected, "Sire, I have confirmed a new blemish on the surface; one certainly not there yesterday."

Without lowering the ax, the King ordered, "Show me!"

"You may not easily see it in this light, though it's there for sure."

The ancient lifted the egg and angled its surface toward the ambient outside light, now trickling in from the early morning sun. True, there it was. The lightest of scratches, not a blemish, certainly not a wound. One so subtle, most would never have seen it. Even on a piece of precious imperial green jade, such an anomaly would hardly constitute a flaw.

What You Saw Was Here

The King looked intently. At first nose close. Then from arm's length. Mulling the anomaly in silence for some time, he then shook his head uncertainly.

"I'll grant you this finding, though I struggle with whether it is new."

"Then I have not corroborated your own finding?"

"Are you suggesting I lied?"

"No sir. I thought you might have been testing me."

"Gads, what a clever fellow," thought the King.

Di Xin stared hard, his penetrating gaze seeming to be scanning for cracks and faults concealed within the ancient one standing before him. "Of course I was testing you. It's part of my art. Pushing hard and always for change, subjecting every aspect of reality to the standard of my judgment, then rearranging it, or reducing it to something else. That's why heaven made me the King; why I'm its very son, and not you."

Even the sage had to think about that. *"What hand could heaven possibly have in all of this?"*

Then, to the old man's considerable relief, the hand wielding the ax relaxed downward.

In fairness, the old man was no coward. He had no fear of death itself. Only the thought of its fast approach unsettled him.

"If what I have shown you has not corroborated your finding, and if indeed your finding be fact, there can be only one other possibility; all trickery aside."

Now the King sensed the intellect of an equal unfolding before him. Smiling, he answered, "Apart from trickery, what other possibility might there be?"

You see, Di Xin had smarts. He had in fact thought he found something. But for once, a rare exception mind you, he questioned even himself. Hence, the need for corroboration.

Of course, the others would look first to where they thought he saw what he saw, and that would be the top of the egg as he set it down. Indeed, what the old man detected lay on the very top, just as it had been set. *"Too easy"* he thought. Still, he saw what he saw, though he sensed something amiss. The King knew what he knew; and what he found wasn't at the top. The sage anticipated trickery going in but found what he found and for a moment let go of his apprehension. But for the two, all in the room were clueless to what was unfolding before them.

Turns out the Sage's discovery did not corroborate what the King saw. Nor could it possibly have done so. In that, there had been trickery indeed. The crafty King saw a flaw, then rolled the egg in his cradling arms turning the flaw away from top to bottom, all done before calling out to the others. A test, and a trick. He expected the old man to find nothing on the top, but somehow, he did. It had eluded even the close scrutiny of Di Xin. *"Savor the moment old man, while you can. You bested me this once."*

Now, his excellency waited expectantly to see what plays the wily old fox had left.

The old man walked to the pedestal and carefully lifted the egg.

In his hands, he rolled it completely over so that top went to bottom, and bottom to top; and then back to where it started, a full circle. He then studied the ends, again lifted the egg and again set it down, reversing poles as he did so, so now the original top lay at bottom. He had already studied the entire surface closely, and at first resisted playing even further into the madman's labyrinth.

But his inquisitiveness bound him onward. You see, that's how it is with sages. Always compelled to sate their curiosity. So thin a line between brilliance and madness.

Just as he was about to scream, "Fuck you, you imbecile!" he noticed something which had eluded his scrutiny earlier. Was it a blemish? A scratch? Was it even there, perhaps a 'floater' somewhere in his eye. Or imagination now claiming its place in this effervescent reality which may or may not be an illusion extending from yet another imagination.

Staring more closely at what had been the bottom, he had to look twice and again, even turning away and blinking his eyes to clarify their focus. Now with his nose almost touching the surface, he attempted what he had not done before. He tried to peer through the surface to what lay within. Not many could have pulled this off. Sages … a different story. It was an exercise he had mastered over a lifetime of looking into himself. Ever deeper, penetrating layer by layer, peeling until he had stripped away the non-essential. As he probed the egg, his intent focused. Directed by his gaze, it came to rest on what now felt to be a resonating heart. Simply there, seemingly neither alive nor dead, yet resonating in his hands. As he concentrated outward, on his hands and the inherent sensitivity of his palms, even they could feel its pulse. Now he wondered where this might lead him. He rolled the egg once again in his grip, returning it to its original orientation, the blemish he first noted once again on top. He set it down on the pedestal and looked more closely. Slowly, he set the fingertips of his right hand onto the surface. He again felt the resonating heart within. There, precisely under the tip of his middle digit. When he traced his fingertips elsewhere, the pulse diminished, then became stronger when his hand returned to the original spot.

He grew aware of what must be happening. The dragon seed within was looking to emerge. It … whatever it was inside, had found the blemish, and probed from within, just as he did from without.

The sage continued exploring, feeling elsewhere on the surface and found nothing, until he again returned to the bottom, now rotating it again to top where his right palm lay quietly and still on its surface.

Now growing impatient, Di Xin ordered, "Quick old man, if you're not up to the task, I'll find someone else who is."

Thoughts of Daji danced in his head. Her insatiable appetite for unbridled morning pleasure had become something he relished at the start of each day. Why not? It worked up a healthy appetite for the morning meal which usually followed close upon. He knew she now waited for him and had already been preparing her vitals. The thought of further delay visibly pained him.

The ancient one stood still as stone, hardly breathing, allowing nothing to interfere with his senses. He moved his hand about. There, now he felt a beat, again beneath his middle finger. His mind marked the spot and this time, as he lifted his hand, he thought he saw the object pulsating, but then instinctively blinked his eyes and shook his head. Whatever he thought he saw had disappeared.

In its place, he found another blemish, one no less subtle than that which he had first uncovered. But was it really there, or had his desire to survive tricked his imagination into deceiving him?

He could scarcely see anything now. He played with it again, angulating the egg this way and that in the light.

"Enough already!" yelled the King, "Guards, remove him!"

Now he saw it clearly, a delicate scrape, evident only in the lightest play of shadow on the undefined coarseness of the abrasion, barely the width of a spider's strand, lit by the morning sun.

As though talking to himself, the sage said, "No need sire, I have completed my study."

He turned to the King, "What you saw was here, beneath the tip of this finger."

He held it forward, exposed, so there would be no doubt.

The others, now irrepressibly curious, began to huddle about. They saw nothing. *"A ruse," they thought.* Their curiosity abated just as quickly. They scampered backwards, none eager to be beneath the spray of red which they expected to erupt immanently.

Di Xin came to where the ancient stood. Without looking to the egg, he eyed the sage and asked, "How can you be so certain?"

"Because you have already ruled out the first. Besides this, I have taken care to confirm there are absolutely no others. This anomaly, hardly a flaw, did not exist before today. Even the egg affirms this."

"The egg, how does it affirm anything?"

"By pushing outward, looking for faults to penetrate, like any entity looking to be born. Your sleight of hand fooled even me sire; I did not expect it, nor did I catch it at first. A test well played. Though it may not have been your intention, not only have we proven your first finding; the discovery of a second only convinces we have made noteworthy progress."

A Riddle Unraveled

"Progress?"

"Yes, the surface can be abraded."

"What do you take me for sage? Of course it can. I knew that all along. But how, with what?"

"By with whatever shaped the stone on your ax sire. Mind you, the egg represents a much more significant challenge, and will take considerable time, but first, you must find those who hold the secrets to this long-neglected art."

The King knew instantly the old man had unraveled the mystery.

"Your price?"

"My price sire?"

"Yes, dammit, what do you want for your service rendered today?"

"Freedom."

"Freedom? Is there such a thing?" Even the King yearned for freedom, knowing each day would begin with his complete surrender to the unfathomable allures of Daji and end with his floundering helplessness as she toyed masterfully with her pleasure puppy. Of course, one might question whether he truly wished to escape from his bondage, so willingly did he carry his chains about. "Where would you go?"

"Not for me sire ..." he turned and faced those again pinned to the walls "For them. They have no further purpose here."

"And you?"

"Do with me as you will."

"Ah, the old bastard saw through me from the start. Why, I'll bet he's even prepared to jump in the stew pot if it'll spring his useless friends."

The sage stood silently and waited patiently for the King's reply. By now, the old man had made his peace with death, a small price against the proposed return.

"Guards," called Da Xin. "Take him!"

The sentries apprehended the sage, no surprise at all to those who watched from the safety of the surrounding walls.

"You know what to do with him!"

The guard Captain affirmed and off they went. Before leaving the chamber, the King turned about almost as an afterthought, quietly ordering the sentries who remained.

"Kill them all, they serve no further purpose. I'll not tolerate uselessness, nor have them blabbing out there about any of this."

His majesty thought he was very clever. The old man didn't want his freedom, and he got it. He wanted to save the others, and he didn't. *"That's why I'm the son of heaven, and you're not. I alone determine the fate of others."*

The Captain had his sentries release the sage at the western gate. As ordered, he gave the old man ten gold sovereigns, a fortune in those times. The sage eyed the Captain, as though inviting an explanation. All he got was, "Head west old man, disappear. Leave no trace. Today, he has set you free. Tomorrow, he may be of different mind. You don't want to return to this living hell."

The old man nodded, appreciating what scant traces remained of the officer's upright character in speaking candidly if only this once. "And the others, young man?"

"What others?" he responded. As if that reply fully sufficed, he turned about and quickly took his leave.

The old man pondered but for a brief moment, before the meaning came clear.

Look there friend, the sage stands frozen, devastated on learning of the slaughter unfolding inside at that very moment.

"*Ah, so much for character. When your very survival depends on whether you are breathing or exhaling in accordance with your master's dictates, where can your true character alight.*"

The old man turned about and started walking west. No fool, he knew exactly what to do. Bank on the unexpected. When Queen Daji heard of his release, she raced to her husband and pined wistfully over her plans to secure their continued pleasure and prolonged lives, perhaps even immortality. Now hopelessly dashed with the old man's ill-considered release. "Remember," she reminded, "We had discussed our intentions on this …" The look on her face left no doubt Di Xin would somehow have to right this situation, or forgo what he needed more than his kingdom, the incandescent rapture only Daji could release within him.

So, he once again summoned the Captain of the guard and ordered he bring the old man back, adding he and his Queen intended to dine with him that very evening before retiring.

Knowing the likelihoods from direct experience, with great regret but much haste, the officer raced to the western gate, where he had just released the old man, and where he fully expected to still find him.

Peering from the portals, he saw only traders, merchants, beggars, and mendicants.

The old man had disappeared, appearing to have completely vanished from where they just liberated him. In disbelief, the Captain ordered a company of men assembled, and to be doubly sure, a second. Before the sun went down, Di Xin had an entire division of ten thousand men scouring the countryside for the old man, who, through sagely sleight of hand, had absconded, and in fact never again countenanced his nemesis Di Xin in that realm.

No doubt, the sage still had a few tricks of his own.

The Captain knew he could not return without the old man, so he too attempted to make his escape before the sour news reached the witch Queen.

Unlike the sage, he of course knew nothing about the art of invisibility nor the transformations, and soon enough found himself in the hands of his once comrades. With great regret, but not so much as to dull their own determination to survive, they delivered him to the King. Fortunately for Di Xin, the young and virile captain proved to be a titillating diversion for the now fully inflamed Queen who immediately locked on to his particular charms and wanted nothing more than to whisk him dutifully away to her private chambers.

"A gift to you my dear," King Di pronounced, all the while smiling broadly at the Captain, "No hard feelings young man, make things right with her, and all will be well between us. Ready yourself for a once in a lifetime experience."

While the King distracted himself with a retinue of newly harvested courtesans, the guards wondered whether the screams emitting from the Queen's chamber were expressions of unbounded pleasure, or cries of abysmal pain. They had heard both many times before but had lost the ability to distinguish one from the other.

In the morning, they received their orders to remove the dissipated body of the once Captain from the Queen's pleasure hive. His corpse now riddled with erotic tattoos, accented throughout by bruises, cuts and punctures seemed almost adolescent in its gleaming innocence. The broad, now permanent though devious grin engraved on his face a lasting testament perhaps to his final thought of getting one over on the King.

Daji took great care to greet her husband warmly, embracing him before all in her full nakedness, proclaiming proudly before the corpse, "As you can see, dearest, we have more than one artist in our midst." She turned to one of her attendants, carefully passing a jade box, instructing, "For my collection, another fine trophy. We may not have gotten longevity (looking ruefully at her mate); but we certainly did receive its full evening's blossom (now smiling appreciatively)."

All stared at the jade box as it whisked away. All knew what lay within.

Di Xin breathed a sigh of relief. *"Back on good terms, thank the heavens!"*

That same day, King Di summoned the artisans, gem cutters, and jade carvers of the realm. The promise, a thousand pieces of gold for whoever knew the ancient secrets of shaping the stone axes from raw corundum. Soon enough, the old craftsmen came forward, proclaiming their expertise in the lost art. But none could demonstrate what they promised as doable. "A paucity of proper materials," they contended.

You see, the secret lay in the abrasive. To shape corundum you needed corundum, better yet, something superior.

"Jade?" asked the King incredulously.

"Diamond" they replied.

You also needed a carefully engineered apparatus. Capable of driving grinding wheels while the egg remained safely cradled, but under constant abrasive assault. Of necessity, one must gauge the range and penetration of the wheels to the final intended result. By the King's decree, "We seek its very essence, the spine within, in the shape of a rod, the same proportions as the handle on a battle mace." He delivered several specimens so there could be no possible error, cautioning, there would be no second chances. The only possible outcome would be success. "Success, or death," he declared.

And so it went, there would be no further impediments, drawbacks, or delays. Whatever it took, he instantly delivered. Out from the royal stores came the kingdom's collection of jewels. As the royal couple beamed incessantly, they knew now, they were onto something. The ministers of state and the general staff witnessed in horror. The straw which dropped the elephant to its knees came when they learned the King had ordered a number of yet unshaped diamonds and sapphires pounded into sand. Those at court already knew he was mad, now there could be no doubt. They stared to one another in abject disbelief, witnessing the hidden and long aggregated wealth of the kingdom destroyed in rapturous glee. To what end? Only the mad couple knew.

But could any of those concerned act on their own behalf, or on the people's behalf?

Not even one.

As to the King, in this instance hardly mad. For once his actions were perfectly rational. It took a bit of time but in the end, the artisans had their abrasive. With that resolved, the King ordered his engineers, in accordance with the artisans' wishes, to design a network of ever turning wheels, where the diamond and sapphire abrasives endlessly worked against the outer surfaces of the egg, reducing and shaping it inward over time. Nimbly guiding it to its intended final form, a phallus like rod destined for installation into the eagerly expectant sphere.

That's Why He's the King

"I take it then, he succeeds?"

"Most certainly," answered Hui, "It took nearly two years, but the long-anticipated day arrived."

"So, in the end, he somehow joined them?"

"In that lies another mystery my friend. The big question remained, 'How to bring them together?' Di Xin seemed to have lost no sleep over it. The craftsmen knew nothing about the sphere of course, and apart from them, just about anyone who did had already vanished. Among those left, the fraternity of assassins watched the King's folly with skepticism, even ridicule. They had, after all, been at this search for generations, and came up with nothing but piles of dust for their efforts. They gave it up as hopeless, satisfied that instead they had a supreme weapon, albeit with finite scope. They viewed it as a kind of poison, a single touch and its target would be instantly gone. Best yet, gone with barely a trace, and never again seen. It suited their nefarious purposes and proved to be a wonderful selling point for their services. Instant disappearance, guaranteed! So, you see now how all prior attempts came to naught, nothing could append to the sphere. It looked to be insoluble, until the fateful day the fortune tellers saw the fire demon and foretold the dragon's egg. Part of their prophecy they kept only for the ears of the King. It had to do with how the two might finally come together."

"And that's the mystery you refer to?"

"Not quite. From the accounts of others, we've learned what happened. How it happened still has no answer."

"Pray tell, continue."

"Legend has it King Di took the now completed shaft to where he kept safe the sphere. Several elders from his inner circle accompanied, none of them really wanting to be witness to yet another depravity, but unable to plead a convincing excuse. From past trials, they knew of the sphere. They too recognized its vast potential, just as they knew of Di Xin's long search to solve the puzzle of attaching a handle which would bring the weapon to its full potency. To a person, they had concluded it a blighted quest never to reach its intended destination. We can only suppose Di Xin would say, "That's why I'm the King, and not them!" Their concern was how to stop the foolishness before it wholly depleted the wealth of the empire and brought ruin. Imagine their surprise when, as they stood before the orb, King Di summoned for his wife. Then together, she to the front, he glued to her rear, their four hands clutching the wand, first holding it erect then extending it outward as if to push the sphere from its pedestal. They closed upon it. Now, nearly touching, it almost seemed the wand grew in length as the orb jelled in urgent expectancy, intent on merging with its long-awaited mate. In an instant, it was over. Almost too mundane to even take in. Before all as witnesses, the pushing wand penetrated deep into the orb, and with that, the ever-present pleas of the orb for its mate, to which all walking the palace confines had grown long accustomed, fell silent."

"They became one on their own?"

"Yes, permanently melded, and in the aftermath, all whispered about the impossible undertaking now accomplished. How quickly they forgot the cost and the sacrifice. Their shrewd minds now looked forward and calculated the anticipated dividends. Greatness for Shang! Few present could disagree, no one else could have achieved success. Though he may have been insane, all concurred when looking at the newly forged assassin's mace, 'That's why he's King, and not us!'

"So aroused by the consummation of their trinity, King Di and Daji fell helplessly to the spell, dropping to the floor in a spasmodic and uncontrolled display of sexual play, all inhibitions now discarded. The cluster of ministers, though not surprised, stood aimless of purpose, embarrassed and bewildered, wanting to leave, but ordered by the King to hold their ground and witness firsthand his intention to harness and tame the now sated sphere."

"A test of the new weapon?" asked Bao Ling.

"You expected otherwise?"

"I can't say I like where this is leaning."

"Neither did they, he called for some of those present to stand front, then ordered them to grasp the handle and lift the mace. They cowered at the thought, already knowing what had happened to others. The King laughed at their reticence, lifted the mace himself by its new handle, then peered deeply into the vast emptiness within the sphere. Daji stood beside him. Then, to everyone's shock and surprise, he held the mace high in his right hand, the orb directly to his front, centered on the line of vision between him and the elders, who stood silent in awed surround.

"And here Bao Ling, we find a clue which answers your question regarding the Black Knight, and his contact with the mace. Di Xin, still grasping the handle with his right, lifted his left hand before the beaming Daji, and slowly extended it forward until his fingertips, touched the surface … "

"And?"

"Nothing happened!"

"Aaahhhhh, the handle is its rein."

"So it would seem. But the demonstration had not concluded."

"Of course not," Bao Ling answered, "Surely it had grown hungry in its long anticipation. Now it demanded appeasement for its longings."

"King Di removed his hand from the sphere, then turned to the elders and called for one to touch it, just as he had done, promising they needn't be fearful. For good reason, most cowered, and could not step forward.

"Assured, perhaps looking for credits with the crown, one of the elders pushed boldly to the front and without hesitation extended his arm frontward to the sphere. Turning to the others, he barked, 'I, for one, support the King, and know he will take us to greatness!'"

Bao Ling laughed, but not in idle humor, "Gone I suppose?"

"Like passing through a door and dropping from a cliff. Nothing remained, all observers froze in horror, but for the wistfully smiling Di Xin. Daji now stood in glee ever so lightly tapping her fingertips together in a show of appreciation, pleading for yet another demonstration.

"Thank you for your kind words, and your sacrifice," said the King to the traces of dust at his feet.

"Di Xin stepped before several of the ministers who had just moments before refused to touch the orb. This time, to their collective relief, he instructed they should not touch it. Standing there, looking at the orb, he signaled for absolute quiet, then listened intently. Apart from the lost elder's voice calling for help, King Di heard nothing, and felt no spell or allure as he wielded the handle. Looking to Daji, he could see her looking lovingly to the orb, its influence obvious, she yet again unmistakably aroused. He extended the mace forward, pointing it toward the closest of the elders. The effect was immediate, he studied as all resistance in the elder melted away, and the innocent, almost childlike residual spirit deep within his marrow timidly edged forward, now assuredly craving whatever was being promised. Overcoming all resistance from his still wary root, his arms and hands lifted, then pushed forward as though to lovingly caress the sphere. You know the rest."

Bao Ling mused for a moment, "Master Li's efforts to resist the Black Knight now seem all the more remarkable."

Abbot Hui continued, "Yes. He barely overcame it. The King, pleading innocent misjudgment on his part; but wishing to test further, grabbed another elder. He put the handle in his grip then stood back. Ahhh, there was the voice again. Now he heard it clearly. And with its enticements came visions of bliss with Daji, and recollections of past lives the three had shared in multitudinous forms, all in anticipation of this moment. She now edged closer, also drawn to its spell. They shared the same thought, why not seize the moment and consummate the trinity, simply become one. They looked at each other; the temptation almost overwhelming. But the sphere had other plans. Their role remained here, for now. Instead, they both witnessed as the sphere cast its line rearward to the elder gripping the handle, whose other hand then involuntarily rose, reaching forward on its own to touch the sparkling globe.

They say he mumbled "'So long as I have the handle secured, I am safe.' Alas, on this point, he erred."

"What happened?"

"Before all, the elder wilted to dust, as the mace slowly descended to the ground, where it came to rest."

The King looked about, "Anyone else wish to try?"

"Their voices froze in their throats, their only thought to get out of the chamber. They say the King continued his experiments for the next several months. Those subsequent trials were likely orchestrated for the entertainment and pleasure of his wife, or perhaps at her urgings. He already knew what he needed to know after that first day. Whoever controlled the handle could transport and engage the device. While grasping the handle, it seemed Di Xin alone was impervious to its touch. This, the soothsayers had made clear to him. Without the handle, he didn't know, nor in the end did he ever want to find out. He had what he needed and was satisfied. As to Daji, the soothsayers said nothing, and for her, the question remained unsettled. Without the support of the oracles, it would remain untested and unsettled until a later time. Elsewhere, word of the mysterious new weapon, and its fathomless power spread outside the palace and passed first throughout the kingdom, and then beyond. Most doubted, others took careful note. Rival kingdoms recognized the threat and weighed what they would need to do to protect themselves from the Shang madman."

Assimilating all he heard, Bao Ling thought a bit, then posited, "So, of all beings, only Di Xin is known to have contacted the sphere and been unaffected. But why? Mysteries yet within mysteries. Do they ever end?" He looked to Hui.

"We must learn to accept them for what they are, and to act accordingly based on what we know for fact. Still, in the end it is Di Xin who remains the great mystery. Why him? Why the fall from greatness? Why the turn to absolute depravity?"

Bao Ling replied, "Perhaps he said it for us already. That's why heaven made him King, and not you or I, or anyone else. I fear hands unseen lay close behind all of this. Still, I don't see how any of it explains the Black Knight."

"We're getting to that," promised Hui.

In Pursuit of Bliss

The next evening passed much as the prior.

After resting a bit, and this time allowing the luxury of a small cooking fire, they conjured a primitive stew from their combined stores then laid back to warm, dry and rest.

Shi-Hui Ke broke the quiet to continue his account of the assassin's mace.

He prefaced by recounting the sage, the ancient who had hoped to free his comrades from the King's deadening grip. On exiting the western gate, he lingered briefly only to learn of their tragic fate. Though he knew the prudence of moving quickly, he hesitated, grappling with the urge to linger. Might there be anything, anything at all to do which mattered? For what seemed another lifetime, he stared blankly at the palace walls as though trying to see through them, weighing all possibilities, rigorously running each thought line to its dry end. Another hopeless situation! When would it ever stop? Seeing no opportunity for purposeful action, he mumbled profanities in resignation, the gravity of despair so profound as to nearly turn his own ancient bones into dust. Standing there amongst the many bustling about, he may have been someone's grandfather, or a mindless uncle; lost or abandoned in the market. Others looked, noted, and moved on, giving him no further thought. In those distressing times, their world was full of such characters. Lives had long ago been reduced to the fundamentals. Exploitation and self-preservation.

Compassion existed only as a wistful thought, elusive in its manifestation—so thorough had Di Xin and Daji been in their devilutions. Knowing he could conjure nothing which mattered, or which could change the moment, he turned resolutely about, and walked away, rooting his determination in one single thought. *"I will be patient. I don't know how, or when, or even why, but someday, I trust this wheel will turn about, and they will stand clear in my sights. Only for that moment, will I linger and kindle my hopes."* Then, relying on the tricks, illusions and devices over which he had mastery, he chose to vanish. Not necessarily leaving; just hanging around to take in what happened next. What he found only added to the weight of his determination.

On hearing this, Bao Ling's thoughts raced to Sying Hao, having witnessed how he managed in fact to completely disappear in the midst of others by carefully manipulating their expectations and veiling his own intent. He wondered if the old man could do the same. Hui answered soon enough.

He spoke of how the old sage walked unnoticed through the very midst of the pursuing troops, who arrived first as squads, then grew to companies, and finally ended as battalions spread across the countryside. Not even a flea could have hidden on that dog.

Yet, he remained right there, standing in their midst. He even saw them bringing in the Captain, who, having failed to recover his prey, faced sure doom. The officer's own foiled escape only added to his woes. Those who apprehended the officer were only that morning his friends, companions and colleagues. He pleaded they let him go, no one would ever know, he would disappear, say nothing to anyone. They simply looked at him and could say nothing more. They didn't have to. He knew their plight. Without the old man, and the Captain also gone, they would be facing the royal cannon, subjected to the whims of the royal couple.

The Captain finally acknowledged their quandary and simply acquiesced, "We are still comrades," he said, and then he forgave them for doing the only thing they could do under the circumstances. Tears fell from their eyes as they led him away. For a moment, the sage thought to assist the ill-starred fellow, but on thinking further knew it would come to naught. Instead, he simply let it play out. Something he had so long ago learned to do when fickle fate rendered havoc into the affairs of men. He felt remorse at his decision, and considered it a failure on his part, one that left a bitter taste until his final day. One can eat crow if served, but swallow? Never! He rationalized how the Captain, to save his own neck, would have given him up in a blink if he stepped into the open and attempted to assist. *How is that different from what I did?"* he questioned himself. *"Am I not letting him take the fate intended for me?"*

What troubled the sage was he didn't know the answer to this, or to anything else anymore. He knew how true men arise only when circumstances are most dire, and what they choose to do in those circumstances often surprises. Perhaps the Captain would have risen to the occasion. *"Now, we'll never know."* he thought as he walked away, disheartened, into the night. "It was only I who could have given him the chance."

Ancients have said, "A friend to everybody is a friend to nobody." One must choose possibilities precisely and strive to maximize one's impact. The ancients referred to this as "leveraging effect by harmonizing with the currents of time and change."

If the price of striking now is prohibitively steep, it is best to wait. Then, strike with everything when the opportunity presents.

Bao Ling remained drawn to the plight of the old sage and wanted to know more about him. He thought of his grandfather, and Iron Hand Gao, and the enigmatic stranger he met so long ago in the shrine to Guan. Men like these would never turn their backs and allow what had happened to go unredressed.

Abbot Hui agreed, begging his friend's patience, "Let's not rush a good tale to a quick conclusion little brother, we have the long night before us."

So, out came the candles; and as the two sat in the warming glow, shadows danced to the flames' baton while the heart of the story filled the space between them.

Hui then continued without breaking the thread, adding how chronicles tell of a great sage who passed unnoticed from under the very nose of King Di and eventually became the quickening spirit leading to his ultimate fall. Now, as Bao Ling learned more, he also sensed there had been some history between the King and the ancient one. Hui prefaced telling how at one time, the sage had been regarded as a sublime strategist within Shang. Would it be too brash to say, perhaps even on the order of a Zhuge Liang. We've all seen what he could do.

On This Point, yet a Fool

"In the early years of the reign, coinciding with the emergence of Daji and the great purge following the unraveled assassination plot, the brainsick King, instructed what few trusted ministers remained to scour the land for a mind capable of quelling the incessant distractions. He had lost trust in his generals and state counselors, and faced mounting threats from rebels, usurpers, and barbarians. He needed a talent and proxy who could free him to his new pursuit. Personal sublimation and transcendence into perfect bliss. He planned to delegate and opt for security. 'I have learned my lessons. The King does what he does. Others will manage the state for him, he will manage them. Fail and I'll have you permanently removed. Succeed and I will exalt you. The King will simply be the King; above everything; and no longer within the reach of their plots, and conspiracies.' He made it so.

"Those whose performance lacked, disappeared inexplicably. The exalted rose closer to the King, even taking up residence within the palace. Hardly a blessing for sure, for within the palace they fell prey to Daji's ever intimidating purview. A perfect monopoly of oppression and control. '*Hey, it produces results!*' he might argue. Most importantly, Di Xin would no longer allow 'distractions' to divert his attention from the sphere, or what he conjectured to be its seeming incarnation in the form of Daji. All else would now come second.

"The search rolled on for nearly a year, extending to all corners of the kingdom. The word went out. Ministers were coming to solicit candidates for King's first counselor. Most men of skill, principle and intelligence scattered for the hills or the desert outlands when they heard. Why willingly become a target? Simply too close to the crazy couple for anyone's comfort. Rumors of the goings on abounded. Though they defied belief, the shrewd silence of those who had survived left no uncertainty regarding likely substance. So, the masters, the sages, the wizards, the righteous and the smart enough for their own good simply went elsewhere. For the roving ministers, it seemed the vast land held only peasants, dogs and pigs. Among themselves they joked about not knowing which of the three would be best suited to serve the daft monarch.

"Then, the lucky day arrived when they nearly tripped upon the very man they sought. As their caravan approached the fateful rendezvous, it rolled unexpectedly to a stop. To its front, in the middle of the road under the mid-day sun, an old man squatted, taking a dump. Those in charge couldn't believe the insolence and dispatched the forward guard to 'learn' the old fool. It turned out he moved like water, flowing in, between and around them as they attempted to capture him. Never engaging them, he moved ever forward until he stood directly before the ranking minister, now also arrived in the front and taking it all in.

"'Is that how you treat your elders in the palace?' he asked.

"'I saw a fool shitting in the road, nearly run over by a royal caravan. Young fool, elder fool, still a fool. Be content you avoided execution. Leave now, before my humor darkens.' was the reply.

"'If that's what you see, then I am staring at an even bigger fool.'

"That only offended and angered the delegate, who demanded, 'Explain!'

"The vagrant continued, chastising the minister before his underlings. It would have been a death wish in the capital. He remonstrated how he had been idling his time for months waiting for their arrival, and just when they come, they nearly run him over as he's taking a crap.

"'Well old fool, how do you expect to be the King's man when you don't have the sense to shit in the bushes?'

"'And where would we be now if I were off in the bushes and your little cocksure train of attendants simply raced by? It's no wonder you haven't found the man you seek. How many sages waiting for you in the roadway do you think you trampled before finding me? How many do you think you passed as they crouched in the bushes?'

"Hearing those words, the minister offered no counter, and no further disrespect. This prickly codger warranted closer scrutiny.

"Changing tactics, he ordered the group set camp for the evening, then invited the sage to dine. There, alongside the roadway in the middle of nowhere, he and his aides conferenced with the old fellow. When they asked his age, he answered he didn't know for certain. Things like that had long ago lost importance to him. He added he could remember back over five hundred years and would agree to round it off at that if they needed a number. They laughed as he said this of course. As he had been speaking earnestly, he puzzled momentarily at what they found amusing. Which made them laugh all the more.

"While the delegates doubted such anomalies occurred, they knew the peasants often spoke of immortals and ancient ones as if they existed in fact. Not only that, in these parts they assured you didn't have to search for long before coming upon one. Fairy tales! Amongst themselves, the minister and his aides agreed the remote countryside and the wastelands sometimes seemed like different worlds from their own. Strange and mysterious things seemed the norm, often spoken of, and sometimes even witnessed or found. As practical men, they wouldn't argue the point. As realists in a harsh world, they deigned to see it for what they felt it was. Just another something to distract simple peasant minds from endless suffering.

"If the old man wanted to be five hundred years old, fine. Could it be any stranger than the goings on in the palace? Before them stood a remarkable physical specimen, old for sure, much like anyone's grandfather might be. Worn and toughened by experience, but still there, robust and with full physical dexterity. Whatever the reality, before night closed upon them, the stranger had proven his knowledge and skills to be of unprecedented breadth. There could be no doubt he had witnessed, influenced, and experienced much.

"At sunrise, as the old man stood like a post, bonding with some resting migrant cranes, they conferenced over what they had stumbled upon. Certainly, the old codger had not been what they had expected, or even hoped to find. To a person, they knew the risks to themselves. *What if the court deems him unsuitable?* In the end what decided them was their weariness of the long travels and endless searching, and their not really having any better alternatives, nor inclinations to push further ahead. The King was not a patient man. They elected to return to the capital with this find, hoping only to keep their heads, which they were certain to lose if they lost more time looking further, or returned empty-handed. Besides, outweighing any of their lingering reservations, the old man had genuinely convinced them of his underlying potential to do the job. In less than a day, he had proven his merit.

"The sage spoke smartly in setting his age by what he could recall with certainty. Sitting in their midst the day before, he eventually had them speechless, recalling events from centuries past as if they had been only yesterday. For them, the coherence of his accounts was incontestable. Their major themes and points matched all existent histories and records, kept close hold in the palace under the diligent eye of the Grand Recorder. No equivalent records existed anywhere else. You either knew what happened firsthand, or you knew what secrets lay in the royal archives.

"On meeting him, the King seemed at first displeased, perhaps suspecting a hoax put on by his own ministers. Or maybe the old fellow had taken them in with his cleverness. He clearly had considerable skill and stores of ammunition with which to spin deceptions over those around him. So, Di Xin decided to play too. Wanting the old man to be clear as to precisely where he stood, the King, acting the polite host, led him by arm on a tour of the palace. Among the highlights were Daji's many tools of persuasion, ending of course with a live, perhaps we should say, not so live, display of the grand brass cannon in action.

"The old man stared disbelieving at the crass display. In all his years, not for a single moment did he ever entertain the thought of humankind descending so low. The King turned to him then whispered softly, as though making a not so thinly veiled threat, 'I will tolerate no jokes between us old man.' Only then did the intimate screening begin.

"King Di, no small intellect himself, challenged the sage for days unending over the arts, the sciences, healing, governing, strategy, the classics, bone reading, and Shang history. The old man knew more of and about his royal ancestors than did even King Di, proving his points with details of the royal lineage only the King himself could have known. When asked how he knew these things, the sage replied he had made the acquaintance of kings in the past, 'Some of your ancestors among them.'

"In the end, there could be no doubt of the old man's qualifications, if not authenticity. What lay uncertain remained his true nature. A very clever man? A spirit? An ancient?

"King Di invited Daji's input in unraveling the enigma. When it came to the mysterious and the boundaries of perception, she, better than anyone, could shake away the fog. Once involved, she studied the elder's dealings with the King closely. She started with the elementary. It was his root which spoke first to her. She observed, 'Simply perfect. Relaxed and impeccably centered, better than any she had ever seen. Not a spirit. Their roots lay elsewhere. Not simply a clever man. Cleverness reaches only so far, and typically folds back onto itself.' An ancient ... for certain. There were many lifetimes evident in the root she saw. At first, she too had been skeptical of this. She had heard stories about immortals but had deemed them myths. Admittedly, her own mentors assured her of their existence; but even they could not swear to having encountered one. Now, she found herself convinced. Trying to win over the still skeptical Di Xin, she rationalized, 'If the sphere can consume souls; can it be any less likely that before us stands an immortal?'

"Hearing this, the King studied, pondered, then in the end begrudged her conclusion. For him, no better explanation existed. Once you have ruled out the likely; then truth must lie with the unlikely. Regardless, the old rascal had the tools for the job, and King Di saw this lone prospect as exceeding all of his expectations going in. He had his Prime Minister.

"In a grand ceremony of assignation, he issued his royal seal to the ancient one, proclaiming his role and authority from that point. Daji took great interest in the old man, never quite deciding whether she feared him, wished to destroy him, or wanted him to be part of her. By now of course, if your instincts had sharpened with what you have learned, you would expect no less of her.

"The sage had originally come forward because he reckoned only he could save the land and redeem the King. On this point, he had truly been a fool; ancient or not. In a way, he was still crapping in the middle of the road as the royal train approached."

Patience, a Fool's Virtue

The palace and capital were rift with purges, disappearances, and wanton exterminations. Nothing ran as it should, nor could it. Adrift in this swarm of goings on, the new Prime Minister found no traction to act with purpose. *"How can I save the land and redeem the King amidst the constant purging of my staff? I waste my days addressing constant airs of suspicion and accusation. All carefully spun by the seemingly everywhere and incessantly meddling Daji. Of necessity, this will come to an eventual head."*

All hours, day or night, she seemed invariably to gravitate to his side. Like a clinging spirit essence, her maddening scents and thinly veiled flirtations enough to drive any lessor man to wild and catastrophic folly.

He hadn't always been celibate. A person of his vast experiences could not help but to have on occasion clung to vines of the finest flowers which time and the realm had to offer. As an honest sage, he once told King Di when asked, "No sire, I have never met even one who can match the exquisite and alluring beauty of Daji. From her glistening hair, streaming perfectly over her exquisite breasts to the perfect comportment of her every aspect. From shape of leg to gray, yellow and blue tints dancing within her inviting eyes, her tongue a flicker ever inviting as words roll like sound of song from her lips. Never in all my years have I seen her equal."

The King beamed on hearing, but already knew all this of course. Still, the sage didn't speak of why he seemed immune to her charms, and this puzzled Di Xin. No one else could resist. There was an explanation for sure, the old one just didn't like talking about it. You see, even though the ancients have their own ways of tricking time; time has a few tricks of its own. You may well discover the secrets of eternal life, but when you take the trip, you'll have to leave some things behind. As the sage learned to his chagrin, after the first hundred years, some things just continued to grow old, even while others went on far beyond their natural measure. Read that as you will. One thing continues, another withers away. At first, the sage considered it a great loss, he had indeed enjoyed it well when he had it.

In recompense, he gained clarity, though it took no small number of years to appreciate it over what he had sacrificed. Perhaps from having touched truth, or perhaps simply conning himself, he now saw all living things as transient— there, but for the moment. The race, the game, the fleeting time where beauty and passion captured the will, would bloom and run their quick course as nature dictated. No trickery, formulation, or incantation would forestall the certain exit. He certainly tried! Where once stood beauty and form, he now found spirit, and sometimes its defining essence. This had been a grand and wondrous revelation. Unfortunately, just as frequently, perhaps even more so, what he found within the spirit-kernel of others proved muddled with silly and irredeemable inclinations. Clouds which in their constancy stormed between the nature of some, and the good of all. As others stood transparent before his sage eyes, he looked first for their root, and within their root, their core; and within their core, their spirit; and within their spirit, any traces of compassion. That grew ever to be his focus. Always find the defining essence. Within Daji, he found nothing; nothing at all. That too stood her out as singular amongst all whom he ever encountered.

But not all went poorly. Despite the impediments, the sabotage, and the paucity of resources, the sage in his transcendent brilliance somehow managed to secure the land, and to repel all threats and invaders. The bedeviled Daji fumed as he even grew the treasury, finding new ways to move water from the flowing valleys to the heretofore uncultivated drylands. For once, there came surpluses. Why even the peasants found occasion to smile, though not often. Still, it represented something. A fresh start? Hope?

It became too much for Daji to bear. Who might this sage really be? What will he target next? Where might his ambitions lead? Indeed, things did come to an eventual head. She declared him a threat and acted decisively to have him removed. She took measures to undermine his growing prominence, his influence, deeds and accomplishments within the realm. It was she or him, she told Di Xin. A choice no man should have to make, let alone a King like the man Di Xin had become. Because he could not lose her, he would have to sacrifice the good of his people.

The re-be-mused King and his witch-wife collaborator insisted on participating in every detail, dismissing the Prime Minister's protestations as envy which she declared as unbecoming to him. He could barely conceal his outrage. The nation accelerated once again into a toxic fog and dissolution of purpose as the two looked on with glee. His only remaining recourse? The sage did what any sage destined to slide the long glowing cannon would do. He saved his hide for another day. With the extirpation of his efforts, and the eradication of his achievements, he descended all too quickly into raving madness, the clear weight of loss too much for any one man to bear. Or so it seemed. All these doings appalled the ministers who first delivered him to the King. For once, they had taken hold of the good, and seen what it might do if empowered and emboldened.

Not quite so easily lulled, a pouting Daji urged that King Di have him sanctified and his essence distilled on the slide of the burning cannon. Enjoying the charade immensely, and for added effect, she even brought the sage before the King. She wanted his thoughts on the proposed cleansing. When faced with the prospect, the now seemingly mad sage jumped for joy at the very thought, begging "Please, please can we do it now? I must be rid of this headache!" pointing to his ass as he said it.

Daji could take no clear read from this. Truly mad, or was he mocking her, perhaps even gaming her? No matter. The self-crowned high priestess of the macabre knew there would be no pleasure or stimulation gleaned from granting the wish of a madman already begging for purification. She would find others more deserving of deliverance. But what to do with him? She yet harbored thoughts of prolonging her own life. He might somehow figure into that. She'd have to think more on this. So, off he went to solitary confinement. Chained sometimes to the floor, perhaps the walls, and when the spirit moved her, to the ceiling. All the while he smiled blissfully. For added good measure, he ofttimes drank his own urine, and even rolled in his own feces, like a puppy scratching its back. She visited often, fascinated at the display, sometimes adding to the moment by bringing the King. At this point, just about anything would arouse them. They say he remained in this state for twenty years. For us, a near eternity. For him, little more than a prolonged detour. But still, a formidable ordeal, even for an ancient. Such can be the price borne for the saving of one's hide. It took all of his wits to survive. As years passed, the King and Queen eventually became convinced of his madness. Nothing hinted to the contrary. Eventually, the initial stimulation waned for them; she couldn't recapture the exhilaration no matter how carefully she manipulated the diorama. For the old one, it had been merely another transformation. In these things, he had consummate skill, and even greater patience. For the royal pair, the encounters proved immensely pleasurable at first. As years passed, they found him less interesting as a diversion, and eventually simply left him alone to his imbecilic solitude, and his keeper.

The Bone Casters Quibble

In a world where evil, treachery, and uncertainty threatened anew each day, Ji Chang, held steadfast and righteous, as once did his grandfather, Danfu, and his martyred father, King Ji[17]. This same spirit reflected even in his uncles, no less gifted or honorable, who, rather than plague the land with discord, voluntarily left Zhou, generously deferring to the obvious talents of their younger brother Ji Li[18]. They agreed to live in exile to the East, where they eventually and independently founded their own flourishing state of Wu[19]. Ji Li, as did his father Danfu, dedicated his reign to finding common ground among the many tribes and factions inhabiting the Wei wilderness, in effect coalescing many smaller bands and once-migrating groups into a formal state. That had been the situation before his betrayal at the hands of the Shang, and the subsequent ascension of Ji Chang as King Wen.

Ji Chang had a keen sense of resolve, guided closely and taught by the examples of both his father and grandfather to rule with justice, tolerance, selflessness and compassion. In

---

[17] Common name Ji Li.

[18] King Ji

[19] Not the same Wu as that ruled in a different time by the Sun clan. This regional kingdom existed approximately seven hundred years before being defeated and assimilated into Yue in 473 BCE.

all of these, he excelled. Encouraged by their prior example, he cultivated talent within himself. And also nurtured likewise among his people and throughout his kingdom. "Always strive for excellence and to better yourself and those around you," insisted his grandfather. "People don't always know it, but more than anything else, they live first to define and actualize who they truly are, and to do so with excellence. The great misfortune of our times makes this pursuit nearly impossible. Hunger and survival push to the front, and forever impede. When your every moment stands defined by the need to make it through the day, what becomes of your more noble purpose? You, grandson, must make the difference. Only you can set the example, and only you can hollow out some small refuge from hard reality where those within can orientate themselves to that special purpose. As leader, it will fall to you to align the people with the Tao, and with its virtue."

To that end, like his father and grandfather before him, King Wen surrounded himself with talented people. Always protecting and encouraging, rather than suspecting and purging. Is it any wonder when one day he stumbled upon a sage who would, through his good office, open the pages of history into a new chapter?

The great historian Sima Qian records how his grandfather had long in advance foretold the meeting. As a young prince, Ji Chang laughed at the old man's reliance on bone readers. But in time, he too studied what the old man learned from them, and acknowledged their value, so long as one weighed carefully what they said and resisted the urge to act from gullibility or fear.

One fateful day, King Wen called his own bone tellers to the royal chamber. Wanting to keep his generals sharp, and to encourage camaraderie, he had decided to undertake a hunt in the remote outlands. On a more practical level, he intended to use the hunt as cover for his cartographers to document and reliably map the strategic details of the vast wilderness. Preferring to leave nothing to chance, he had asked the court readers to forecast his prospects for success. They cast their bones and pulled their sacred tortoise shells, tossed their yarrow stalks, blew their smoke, and poked their tea leaves. And then of course they charted the skies, studying closely for meaning among the diverse emerging patterns. Trying to make sense of it all, they stared speechless in what seemed confusion, and then in wonder. That quickly drew the King's interest!

At first, he waited deferentially as they conferred, allowing them adequate time to reach consensus. He then found his patience tested as they argued over the augury. Finally, worn thin by the incessant delay, he ordered them to stop their bickering and give up their findings. "While you bone shakers continue your squabbling, I can decide what they mean for myself, and get on with the hunt! You have my royal permission to hold your summary until I return. Then we can compare your forecast with what actually happened. What could be better than that?" They pleaded for more time, insisting he not dismiss such anomalies lightly. "Be patient sire, we will not fail you." He quipped how his beard would be touching the ground before they ever finished. "Spill out what you have!" he ordered.

And they did, saying what they could. The hunt promised to be auspicious and would prove successful. But not because he would bag any particular prey of note. Their confusion grew evident as they struggled for the words, "It would be the other way around." they said, almost too embarrassed to continue. Eyes lowered in deference as they added, "Imagine you are the prey. Not unlike a fish about to come upon a hook."

The King's demeanor grew incredulous. "You mean I'll be stepping into someone's trap?"

As they continued, laboring to make sense from what appeared to be utterly contradictory. He listened even more intently while they labored to articulate the core of their confusion. The trophy of his hunt would be a man. One sent to him from times past to guide him, his children, and his grandchildren into a future of great prosperity and influence. But this man, a sage perhaps, unambiguously showed in the bones to be the hunter, and not King Wen. "Sire, it would seem he has been searching for you or one like you for some time … as of yet, to no avail."

"Now you deliver me impossible riddles to decipher. Anyone can make this stuff up. I'm the hunter. I'm the prey. Whatever happens in this confusing mess, in the end, you'll doubtless claim having foreseen it!"

Then he smiled at them, "Friends, just tell me, now, what this all means, let's not wait until the horse has run the course. Give me your best shot. On that, I will judge and reward your skill."

They could add nothing. Embarrassed and silent, they offered no more.

Curiosity Outweighs Madness

Having feigned madness for so long, the sage sometimes lost track of where the line between the real him ended, and the mad him began. Had he in fact been an ancient, or had that simply been part of the feigned delirium? He had to admit, it was getting harder to tell. Now it seemed he existed only in dream chambers, stepping from one to the next, some of madness, some of great perception. He may well have gotten forever mislaid, but for his assigned warden and keeper, who at notable risk took it upon himself to look after the old fool.

By then, King Di hadn't thought of the old man for years. The riddle of the dragon's egg demanded the King's ceaseless attention. Even with that, the riddle continued to resist all prospects for solution. In moments of profound frustration, he could not help but think upon the madman. The pet sage whom he kept chained and who once proved such a pleasurable distraction from life's profusion of demands and problems. *"Gosh, he had been so good back in the beginning. Perchance I could somehow just return him to his senses, if only for helping with this. We've tried everything else, why not? It might change the outcome. How easy it is to find a thousand opinions, how hard to find among them a single solution. The sage I knew in the beginning would have cut right through the bullshit."* He clung to the thought. The hope, if you will, that everything stood ready, perhaps waiting only for the east wind to push all into alignment, or for the right mind. So, when discretion and opportunity allowed, Di Xin again found himself stealing discreetly into the confine. These times, by choice, he went alone. Appalled, he found the old man at times catatonic and unresponsive. *"It seems we have destroyed him."* Despite his careful precautions, Daji still seemed to know King Di's every move. Perhaps she had eyes in the walls. But even she recognized they had hit an impasse on the egg, and for once, loosened the rein on King Di.

Alone in the cell, he would speak to the mad sage. Just as we are talking now, though more one sided of necessity. He told of the egg. How it related to some unspecified divine purpose and how the bone readers had foretold it. And then he confessed how years had gone by with no progress of any discernible note, which baffled him to no end. The prophets had left no uncertainty that destiny itself had summoned him to the task and had in fact ordained he would succeed. Yet, he saw no way to do so, or where to go next. Neither could anyone else.

At first, the sage held his silence, just staring away and picking his nose, babbling incessantly amidst punctuations of animal noises and random screams. For diversion, he would time his rants to the cries of others in cells adjoining, even howling with them in symphony, like a band of mad coyotes on a moonstruck night.

It was the centuries driven hungering of his underlying insatiable curiosity which finally turned him. Of the faculties which lingered most stubbornly among the ancients, curiosity gripped tightest. As the sage had come to sense, it even grew stronger with time, and was not at all like those things which departed or withered after the first few hundred years. In the head of a sage striving to manifest perfect madness, curiosity might indeed be considered a flaw, perhaps even fatal. You see, one cannot be genuinely curious, and truly mad.

Ask any cat.

There it lay, irresistibly wedging open the door to his vulnerability. He simply had to know more about that damn dragon's egg. So, one day, in the midst of the King's once again rattling off about it to himself, the sage silenced his own babbling. Then, perhaps for dramatic effect, he called out, "Do you think it would help if I saw it."

Make no mistake. He would not serve this master, nor would he do his dirty work. At least that was his thought. News of the assassination of the righteous uncle Bi Gan had reached even his secluded ears long ago. Just as the King was doing now, his warden and keeper often spent time with him inside the cell, thinking he was talking to a vulnerable but once noble madman. In fraternity with the old man's plight, the keeper one day proclaimed, "You and I are the only two sane people left in the kingdom! The whole lot of them have gone batty!" He was doubtless a goodly man. Were it not for his smuggling in and on occasion sharing real food, the sage would long ago have perished. One fateful day, he entered, particularly despondent, proclaiming, "We are lost, even hell will not have us with this atrocity on our accounts." The sage crawled about on all fours continuing to nibble insects while his warden dashed whatever hope remained he might somehow rehabilitate the King. We've mentioned the pull of curiosity. Here too, the sage couldn't resist. He dropped all pretense, then suggested they talk about it while sharing the roasted duck his keeper was holding. Shocked at the sudden transformation, the guard stared hard at the ancient, then could only mumble, "It figures!" Suggesting they forgo any further pretense, he motioned for the sage to come alongside, where, as they ate, he told of Bi Gan's assassination.

"I was there" he said. "The King had first ordered I make ready for another prisoner. I even imagined he'd end up in here with you. As a warning for him to get in line you might say. The three of us would have had a grand time together, an island of sanity in a sea of lunacy. But it was not to be. I remained hopeful until the last moment. You see, to my eyes, for a fleeting moment it seemed his uncle's candor had struck home, possibly even persuaded the King. Who knew where it would go? Mind you, I loved this King when he first ascended as a man in full bloom. The potential for greatness radiated from his every pore, you had to be there to fully appreciate the staggering degree of decline evident in what he has become. Why, he could have been a god! How wretched and rotted have the times become. Our reality has gone sideways; nothing counts to be as it seems. Sure enough, as I stood dumbfounded, yet hopeful, the witch entered the hall, and whispered some sort of incantation into the King's ear. Believe me on this, when she backed away, I thought I saw embers glowing inside his head. Even I, a lowly dungeoneer, could see the change come over him. Then the order rendered from his lips. Cut the still beating heart from the noble uncle and return it immediately. He dispatched the headsman of his own guard, but not until after we all bore witness to the blasphemous display by the witch before our very eyes. I refuse to repeat or describe it even now.

"The two of them wanted to see what the beating heart of a sage looked like! Can you believe we have come to this? That mankind has come to this? That no one present expressed revulsion at the thought? Not even I. We all simply cowered in our terror. Thinking only of ourselves, we abandoned the futures of our children. We should have found the courage to form our own consensus, if only from righteous instinct, and killed them both. Right there where they stood. I will curse myself to my dying day for this ineptitude. Bi Gan was a courageous and noble man. He deserved better from me, from all of us. To his credit, at first even the Captain questioned the order, doubtless he couldn't believe what he thought the King had said. But the King left no mistaking as to his intent. The Captain still balked, but he could not match the wile and determination of the voluptuous Daji. Show me the man who can? I will proclaim that man our savior! In an instant he went racing after Bi Gan, returning almost as quickly. Why, we had hardly even shifted our discomfited weight, as we stood stricken, unable to think, let alone act. The daunting horror seemed to stop time itself. On returning, the Captain dropped kneeling before the King and lifted his hands, and I swear, I saw the still beating heart pulsing as the King gawked at it stupefied. He did nothing else, nor could he. Frozen like us was he. Daji sprung like a panther, her appetite unrestrainable, and before all present sank her teeth into the dripping meat, smiling ravenously as she consumed it piece by piece, stopping only for opportunity to offer fair portion to her beloved. For reasons known only to him, he could not share or delight in her feast. 'No matter,' she said, 'I will eat for both of us.' And so, she did."

Part 2

Ji Chang of Zhou

Dharma's Certain Course

Bao Ling lay speechless, now coming to realize the horrors he had witnessed in his own past were merely an extension of some protracted line of causality, reaching from long before.

Hui continued, "Well, as you already know, the sage did solve the mystery of the egg. He thought it at first to be merely a challenge. One in which if he proved successful, he might gain leverage to accomplish something positive. On learning of its ultimate use, and its role in the finalization of the Assassin's Mace, he judged he had once again erred terribly. 'Do no harm!' That should be a sage's first thought before undertaking any endeavor. Folks like you and I, regular folks are what I mean, when we screw up, the world doesn't turn inside out. When a sage fucks up, there's no telling how bad it can get, or where and when the suffering will end. Worse still, despite their hopes and altruism, they never seem able to undo the mess they leave everyone in. It's no wonder they take to the hills, or the barrens, or sit and stare at walls for decades. Better than anyone, they know the importance of restraint. Ah, but then again, there's the matter of their curiosity. Once seeing the impact of their missteps, one needn't puzzle long over why sages leave kings. You simply can't predict what kings will do, nor can you second guess them, nor can you trust their righteous nature; if it were ever there in the first place."

Bao Ling thought again of Sying Hao as Shi-Hui Ke went on.

"So, when he made his final escape from the madhouse, he did what any sage would do to ensure the return of his sanity. He went fishing and spent his days sitting quietly. 'Fishing?' you may ask. Yes, he wandered into the wilderness alone, looking for a place to his liking, scouring the most remote and idyllic streams, ultimately setting humble domicile on one of the offshoots of the Wei river. There he fished and waited.

"Waited for what?" asked a now confounded Bao Ling.

"We know from accounts left by others, of an odd old fellow who fished his days away. Politely speaking to and rendering genial conversation and advice to anyone who happened upon him. Some even stopped or showed more than mere polite interest, curious and making sure to linger and glean some of what the old codger freely disseminated. Hard earned wisdom. He in return would cautiously partake of their invitations to tea and some victuals politely offered alongside. We're told he rarely ate the fish which he himself caught, and but for the generosity of others, might not have eaten at all. Among those rare passersby would be some who mocked his efforts, though taking care not to ridicule or insult. Clearly the old fellow had smarts, why risk giving offense. Those who coursed the wilderness knew not to take chances. He might very well be a river spirit luring the hapless to some unfathomable end.

You see, he didn't even set a hook to his lines. So, feigning respect and interest, they politely asked for his explanation, wanting to understand the subtleties of his technique. He told them he preferred waiting for the fish to come to him on their own, explaining he had taken many years to perfect his method, though it might yet seem unusual to some. 'When they are ready for me, they will come,' he explained. Well, clearly he had been eating or getting his nourishment somehow. For an older guy, he seemed quite robust. So, in a roundabout way, the fish, only of a different sort, were finding their way to him, and in showing pity to the old man, strangers made sure he didn't starve.

"He remained there in the Wei Valley, in the unoccupied wasteland between Shang and the fledgling kingdom of Zhou, at that time headed by King Wen. That is where the story turns, and the old man's patience reaps its rewards."

Zhou had been a small state embracing the Wei River basin. Despite its smaller size and remoteness, it prospered and grew strong, which of course drew the attention and concern of the adjoining Shang. They saw Zhou to be a vassal state. Ji Chang, better known as King Wen, ruled Zhou. While he ruled benevolently and with a fatherly hand, he knew full well the goings on in his much larger and more powerful neighbor. By now, there were no secrets regarding Di Xin and Daji; accounts of atrocities had become the norm in all news and intelligence reports from Shang. That, and the seemingly never-ending exodus of starving peasants now taxing the resources of Zhou, and the other outlying princedoms. King Wen's own father, Ji Li, known to us as King Ji, had been a loyal vassal to the then Shang King. After conquering and assimilating the surrounding tribes and lessor kingdoms into Shang's domain, King Ji gained great fame and notoriety, which as you may suspect, is never a good recipe for long life under maniacal dictators. His lord, King Wen Ding of Shang (Grandfather to Di Xin) made sure to reward and honor his many accomplishments, just before finalizing his martyrdom.

As his son and successor, King Wen knew to remain ever wary, focusing his great talents everywhere within his own domain. He gave the Shang ample calculated respect and distance, while studying them closely. No fool, he knew he could not match them blow for blow and survive. So, despite their troubled history, and never forgetting the fate of his father, he bided time, and planned to let the rot from within Shang extract its toll before contemplating anything further. Besides, his spies had corroborated what he had suspected from other sources. The mad Di Xin of Shang had come into possession of a fearsome weapon, which no one seemed able to explain or even confirm having witnessed, but of which existence they had no doubt. Only the unmistakable evidence King Di had staked his entire kingdom on the chase made any news of the mysterious weapon credible.

And it is here where the roll of destiny's wheel turns what appears to us as mere coincidence into yet another manifestation of Dharma's own true course.

A Meeting Long Foretold

His grandfather had first voiced the prediction.

Duke Danfu had been a formidable leader. To spare his people from needless warring with neighboring entities, he led them into the foreboding Wei River basin. A wilderness deemed uninhabitable, a challenge for fools. That's what his detractors thought - *Doomed to failure, we'll pick the pieces when he's gone.* Surprising skeptics, he and his followers overcame all obstacles. The community grew, then flourished. More came to join and received warm welcomes. No one had ever seen anything like it. Their embryonic collective expanded outward, eventually encompassing what had been the constantly bickering primitives. Together, peacefully, they consolidated all into one single state - Zhou.

As was the case with all in his bloodline, Duke Danfu possessed a considerable gift for the art of prognostication. For a vehicle, he preferred engaging the ancient methods as passed to him from his forebears: casting bones, reading tortoise shells, interpreting dreams.

Just as he predicted success for his people in the wilderness, he further prophesied the rising kingdom would become strong and prominent under his son and grandson. He further dreamt his grandson would one day happen upon a great sage; one who would profoundly influence the family's destiny. He never said whether it would be for the better or worse; just that it would happen. So certain had he been of these things, he ordered the prediction preserved in the royal annals of his reign.

The grandson, King Wen, wasn't sure he wanted to hear any of this. Either way, the portent rang ominously. It pitted his kingdom against the mighty Shang. If he was the prey, so be it. He knew full well how to defend himself. But to him, a most practical man, any future hinting of great prosperity and influence ultimately pointed to a showdown with Shang. How could that be good for Zhou? Would not the lingering jackals of war pounce on an ascendant Zhou? What of the unmentioned prospects for untold suffering? Of what use are prosperity and influence should tragedy be the final outcome? He knew full well, the unpredictable King Di Xin wanted vassals, preferably docile; and not partners, or rising threats.

True, he held close the memory of his father's unjust assassination. He too had once been their hostage, under threat of the same end. Simply said, his aspirations for Zhou seemed in their very nature to necessitate a showdown with Shang. Though he seldom spoke the words, they had become his oft recited personal mantra. "If I could, I would." Meaning of course, he reserved the right, the privilege, and the very call of honor to avenge his father's death. But he was a patient man. One who standing on the shoulders and accomplishments of his grandfather, and then of his father, had nurtured and grown a fine kingdom from a once insignificant outpost.

Now, with each day, it pushed outward in all directions, becoming ever more prosperous and stronger. Even to the point of assimilating the influx of Shang's destitute, ever streaming through the porous wilderness borders. His close inner council suspected he had oft weighed the prospects of confronting Shang, always in the end deciding against. Even with its problems, and the spreading discontent, Shang remained strong. Moving on them now held less prospects for success than a cat clawing away on the back of an elephant. The effort would only draw the rage of an angered behemoth their way. He would not willingly or through fault of ambition or even carelessness bring misery onto the backs of his people. For now, he would tend to them, grow and push them toward individual perfection. That would be his ambition. A nation of actualized humans, a people who knew themselves. And who, with the value implicit, would stand united against all and whatever threatened. First the one, then the other. Vengeance must wait. Reversing the order spelled ruin. Grandfather had made sure he understood how every moment has its center, its balance, and its root. To own the moment, use timing and precise commitment to find where balance sits. Until you know that spot, be cautious.

So, for now, he would let Shang simmer in its own delirium. As ruler of Zhou, he would try not to draw their unwanted attention, and work to stay out of their sights. Granted, what must be must be, and what must happen must happen. He had no doubt, once freed of distractions elsewhere, Shang would turn its lewd gaze toward Zhou. His own studies into the bones and oracles counseled only patience but promised nothing in return. In that sense, he read and interpreted no better than his own bone casters. So, until now, he had bided time, and within himself perfected patience.

Uncertainty aside, one thing caught his notice. Their prediction regarding the hunt resonated perfectly with the once prophecy of his grandfather, of which these soothsayers had no clue. They spoke of an imminent meeting with a great sage but could add nothing further. It made no sense. What might any sage have to do with a royal hunt in the most remote wilderness?

Ji Chang knew to respect coincidence; the more unlikely the coincidence, the more deserving of one's regard. If destiny should whisper twice in the same ear, only a fool would choose not to hear. So, in preparation for this hunt, he readied much more carefully than usual, undertaking the customary rites of ablution and cleansing, then making additional offerings as appropriate to success in new endeavors. And for added measure, even lifting the annual rice tax from his people. In this, he re-secured their hope, loyalty, and continued trust. Best to enter the future stepping one's foot firmly forward with essential nature intact.

Now several weeks into the hunt, which as it turned out, proved to be quite productive from the very start, his train passed into a remote and uncharted wetland where they found a solitary primitive shack. There in the misty distance, it stood uncertainly on stilts. To the untrained eye, it might seem as though a passing gust should likely drop the shack into the mud below. But Wen saw the cleverness of the geometry. When his aids mocked the structure, he turned to admonish, "Don't speak too soon. That frail shack will likely still be here long after we have all departed." He took care to explain what he saw in its carefully thought-out lines, and how they worked in concert to effortlessly disburse any degree of wind or attack of elements. That quieted their ridicule as their own eyes studied closely to find what had been so apparent to their wise King. Proximate to the shack, an old man sat along the bank of a stream fishing intently. Seeming not to even notice, or perhaps to ignore, the sizable caravan passing to his rear.

So taken by the cleverness of the shack, King Wen observed the old man with curiosity. *"I wonder if he'd indulge me in discussing the secrets of his wondrous structure."*

Now three weeks into the excursion, his stores nearly filled, and still no sign of prophecies waiting fulfillment, Ji Chang welcomed the distraction. He ordered the caravan to continue forward, instructing they set up camp along the hillside to their front, ensuring no unnecessary disturbance to the old man's tranquility. He would follow later. Relishing the opportunity for diversion, he ordered his attendants bring some victuals for him to share with the stranger by the water's edge.

Now alone, he made his way over and came up on the old fellow, "Catch anything?"

"Not yet."

"How long have you been fishing?"

"Oh, hard to say. Honestly, I lose track, I'd have to say several years."

"And you haven't caught anything?"

"Nope, not yet. It's no loss though, I'm a very patient man, and sitting here brings a degree of contentment as I work to quiet my troubled spirit."

"You hardly look troubled my friend."

The old man turned, then answered, "I have come here from Shang."

"Oh," King Wen struggled with what to say next, then added, "Not much opportunity to fish over there."

"You can fish all right, it's just that the bastards won't let you keep them. Worse yet, they might mistake you for practice dummies while they test their new swords." As he said this, Wen noticed what he thought to be a playful twinkle in the corners of the old fellow's eyes.

"You exude great patience. I would have given up long before, perhaps after the first year." He smiled to himself as he said this, wondering if the old man picked up on his attempt at humor, then felt a bit embarrassed as the recluse stared with mock disapproval, clearly having caught him in the act.

The sage turned fully, using the moment to study his guest closely. Just then, the attendants came with their servings.

"I hope you don't mind joining as I pause to dine. I will consider it an honor if you share your true purpose. And perhaps your unique insights into patience, something I work hard at, but stumble frequently."

The old man consented. He begged just a moment to rest his pole on some stakes nearby, where they both could keep a wary eye on any unlikely signs of activity.

"You have quite a hunting party. Might you be a prince, or general? Or perhaps some very wealthy merchant on holiday?"

"First, allow me the honor of introducing myself. My humble family name is Ji, my common name Chang."

"Ah, Ji Chang, honorable son of Ji Li, no doubt. Your father spoke highly of you. King Ji, no finer man in all the territories. His loss, a tragic and pathetic waste."

It Seems I Have Caught a Big One

These words almost flattened King Wen, who by then was an older man himself. He had been but a young prince ascending to his prime when he lost his father. As an unlikely vassal, King Ji had served the Shang with distinction. Over a period of years, he succeeded in quelling the rebellious northern tribes. He had hoped by being a loyal servant and competent general, he would earn the trust of the Shang, and in that, secure the safety of his family and realm. But with the Shang, any display of great valor raised questions, and drew unhealthy attention, more so if attached to victories and successes where all others before had failed. Unfair though it might seem, the unwanted attention often bred suspicions. So it was with Ji Li. It cost him his life, but in the end, it didn't stop with that. Misgivings against the father passed quickly to the son. Worse yet, the question of what the son might do? Did he know the truth of his father's end? Would he not as a filial son seek to redress the loss of a father? Were any kings of Shang safe so long as he breathed?

So, King Wen came to know well the bitter taste of Shang's treachery, "I am who I am, they will not spare me." His father now long gone, Wen worked tirelessly to grow Zhou into the form and stature envisioned by his father and grandfather. Coming into prominence of his own, it surprised no one when the freshly ascended Shang ruler, Di

Xin, summoned Wen to the imperial court. Supposedly to discuss grand strategy and neighborly politics. Di Xin, still reeling from the unforeseen attempt on his own life had already partnered with Daji. In short order, Wen found himself falsely charged with being one of the conspirators. As the accusations unfurled, he had at first been involuntarily detained, and then imprisoned without justification or proof of fault. At Daji's urging, King Di, now seeing enemies everywhere, had lost his senses to where he indeed considered Wen for a slide down the royal cannon. It was the nobles of Zhou who deterred him in the end. They united and staked their fortunes—even their own daughters as ransom for their beloved prince. Their sacrifice changed history; all would have ended had they not paid this terrible price. At the last moment, Di Xin relented, finding the bargain, and the collection of virgins, too enticing.

Wen found the price extracted for his life to have exceeded all measure; and the guilt of the cost and the sacrifice forced upon innocent others weighed on him until his final days.

Vowing to never have this repeat, King Wen dedicated what remained of his life to the overthrow of Di Xin, and with him, Shang. It had been a long and tortuous wait thus far. Granted, Zhou prospered and grew; yet Shang remained a powerful colossus, albeit diseased and rotted within.

The words of the old man before him brought fresh again the memories of his beloved father, and the deceit implicit in his warrantless execution. Wen almost felt anger toward the hermit for pricking this well of pain and allowing it to spring once more to the surface. Fortunately, justice and humanity prevailed. He struggled within to restrain himself, knowing the old man had acted in earnest, and honorably, wanting only to share his thoughts.

"Yes. My honorable father. So many years have passed since we lost him. Yet he remains always in my thoughts. There's not a thing I do where I do not hear his voice, ever guiding my course and purpose."

The sage could only nod his head in acquiescence, "You will do well to mind that voice."

"And may I ask in turn, what is your honorable name good sir?"

"I am Jiang Ziya, known by others as the grand inept fisherman of the Wei river basin."

The name meant nothing to King Wen, though somewhere within, he thought to have heard it in the past.

"The honor is mine venerable fisherman. Did you perchance know my father?"

"Yes, I knew him well enough, and to value what he strove to be."

The old man could have said much more. He might even have told how he was there when they killed him. Standing among a crowd of stunned onlookers. Witnessing as the sovereign's own palace guard, disguised as rebels, brazenly murdered their state hero. The rebel masquerade had deceived the throng, but not the sage. For Jiang Ziya, yet another instance where he stood helpless and frozen before incomprehensible treachery.

"Just as I sit with you today, he once welcomed me to his table. We talked of our differing stations in life. He, most intent on learning how the commoners fared in Shang. He expressed hopes his recent victories would bring lasting peace. Thus, freeing the nation's resources to better serve the people. He recounted his own father, and the elder brothers he loved, who removed themselves from Zhou rather than impede his own ascent to rule. Then he spoke of his love for you, and your noble brother, as well as your siblings, and the confidence he had in you both, that you would actualize all the aspirations of your ancestors and in due time nurture Zhou to its full prominence. He also talked of his hopes for a day when no despots or neighbors of uncertain design, indubitably meaning Shang of course, could enslave it."

"You do know my friend, even here, in the middle of nowhere, words like that would be viewed as treasonous to a Shang sympathizer?"

"Yes, but I speak only to the honorable Ji Chang and no others. Elsewhere, perhaps better to be a raving madman than to draw undue attention with the truth." The old man smirked; the irony evident in his demeanor. That told Ji Chang much more, perhaps, than did his words. He had heard rumors once of a madman, kept almost as a pet, by Di Xin and his wife.

"Unless joined by another madman," laughed Ji Chang, "Two fools bantering as friends. Only then might truth find perfect sanctuary."

The sage smiled, "Agreed! The ignored space between two madmen in these crazed times. Only truth will pass between them. Shall that be us? Two fools sharing a rod which catches no fish. I say 'Yes!' as I wave my saber of swamp straw. Let the wrongdoers sneak, lie, steal, torment and deceive. We will piss in the face of the power they hope to weigh upon us. Truth takes best root in patience, and arrogant fools have no use for that, or for the passage of time. In the cycle of Yin and Yang, all dogs will have their day; that includes the mad ones. Nothing stands permanent. When the cankered mist of chaos clears, and one gapes to see what caused it to lift, he will find little else besides patience, compassion, and dharma; oh, and fearlessness of course. Can't get anywhere without that. Stuck in time, ill doers will gnash their teeth as their short-lived day comes to its certain end. All their plots, deceits and manipulations leading to naught. Imagine their last thoughts when the poisoned fruit rendered by their interminable plots and deceptions survives all their purges of righteousness and returns like a great flood flushing away all which they were, and which they held at dear cost over the heads of countless others."

"Judging by his countenance, and his very commanding craft of words, the old man before me hints at a much broader chronicle. Much more than that of a simple hermit unable to catch a single fish; or might that too be part of some very subtle game." Ji Chang thanked the old man for sharing his father's words, proving no ambivalence as to King Ji's character, or the clarity of his thoughts and wishes even on nearing his unanticipated end. In his own heart, King Wen banked all of it to be true, dismissing any thought of deceit from the old man. It was how he remembered the past, a father's love, a family's nurturing, his careful upbringing. King Ji had sought out and recruited the finest teachers, all of one mind in directing the child prince. Accept no compromise in the pursuit of excellence. The wise father spared nothing, seeming always to know the future lay just beyond his own dreams. And always, in all things, and in all ways, the people of Zhou came first; and just as certain, close after them the betterment of humankind.

They talked, idled and ate. Though the old fellow said little more of himself, King Wen found him to be a very learned man. Even on occasion offering casual insights into strategy which Wen found to be nothing short of brilliant.

For both, it was with no small degree of sadness and regret that their rendezvous would necessarily soon draw to its close. The attendants timidly approached, reminding their sovereign of the time, and after clearing the table and fare, left Ji Chang to stare absorbedly at the old sage.

"I will remember how you recalled for me in your account of 'fishing,' the lesson of patience."

"Aaahhhh, so you understood that. I suppose one can conceive of situations where advisers might not propose patience, though I can think of none at this moment. As I'm sure you recognize, one can appear patient on one front, all the while laying careful foundation and groundwork on another. Almost like building a trap for a most ferocious beast, one so fierce even the smallest miscalculation ends in disaster. In situations where there can be no error, remember to plan carefully, execute meticulously, and never rush or force your hand. Stick to these principles and your nose will not get bloodied. Whatever you do, leave nothing to chance which is not rightfully chance's domain. Work for victory, but don't crave it; expect defeat in every shadow, and plan accordingly. You will see soon enough how this produces extraordinary results."

Ji Chang marveled at the words, were they directed specifically to him or had the stranger been speaking in generalities? Perhaps the old man meant this to be a message? In the end, all he could offer in response was, "I truly enjoyed our time together, and surprisingly, am greatly saddened on taking leave."

"I too found this time well spent. Now I see the truth in what they say of you."

"What might that be?"

"That you are your father's son."

Ji Chang had no response to that. For him, the sage had conferred the highest of honors. He needed never to have another. The words swept away his composure. It felt as though a clog of wool had lodged in his throat. He could hardly take in air. Sitting there quietly in that moment; relishing memories of times with his father. Suddenly, his attention shot to the old man's rod which had dropped unexpectedly from its delicate perch.

"I think you've finally got one" he raced to the pole, but on lifting it, found no resistance. Whatever caused it to jump, most likely had already made its escape.

"Looks like it got away. Here, I'll re-bait your line."

Laying the pole down, he pulled the line back to the bank's edge and saw only a weighted shank, with no barb.

"Why there's no barb on here. It's no wonder you haven't been catching fish."

Studying King Wen, now holding the barbless shank in his fingers; feigning puzzlement at the finding, the sage lifted the bamboo pole from the bank, then stared down the now taught line to where it ended at the shank, still firmly in the King's grip.

"Haven't I?"

The King stood at a loss, *"What the hell does that mean?"* Only then did the words of his grandfather, and those of his soothsayers all flood his consciousness as he stared back to the old man, now pulling the cord as though playing a fish on the end of a line.

And in some inexplicable, yet enchanting way, it all made perfect sense.

The sage smiled at King Wen, "It seems I have caught a big one!"

In This Affair Patience Must Rule

Ji Chang, eminent King Wen of Zhou, now smiling broadly, would have been the first to agree, but in the background, he saw his attendants laughing raucously at the less than regal spectacle. Understand, some monarchs, with their grandiose sense of self image and warped expectations of deference, would not have taken kindly to a prank like this.

Fortunately for all, this King had a sense of humor far more encompassing than his sense of self. The sage saw this and read it as an exceptionally good omen.

Now, with the prophecy met, the King declared the hunt successfully concluded. He ordered his entourage to prepare for returning to the capital at morning's first light.

That evening He made it a point to linger alongside the riverbank. He and the sage watched the stars slowly passing overhead. Throughout the night, in the glow of a humble campfire, they conversed about affairs of state and the future of Zhou.

As the hours passed, and dawn's first light nudged the eastern horizon, Ji Chang hinted he might have a place for the old man back at the palace. "Why, you'd make a fine minister; and, and you'd have a warm bed, and regular meals. And if you want to fish, we have lakes and moats brimming with wily prospects. Of course, you'd have to start using hooks."

Though at first demurring, he did after all have hard experience in how these things might turn out, the old sage eventually agreed to Wen's kindly persuasions. The entourage had no clue what to make of the odd fellow. Particularly when the King insisted the ill groomed and wild-eyed guest join him in the royal coach, leading the head of the procession. But the great surprise came on arrival at the palace, when at King Wen's behest, the stranger received the ceremonial welcome due a visiting prince.

Only when sharing the return ride in the coach did the King learn at last the stranger's ancestral name, and of his troubled past in the kingdom of Shang.

He had been known as Lu Shang, but it could have been anything. You see, among the ancients, names were simply sounds, pliable and adaptable to the demands of the moment. Their vibrations and the impact of their resonance far more important than any attribution to family or lineage. More often than not, the energy of names chosen far outlived those who came to bear or to know them. An ancient might choose to be known by more than one name, or to undertake a succession of different names. Or perhaps transform into different persons or deemed never to have existed in the first place. Little more than a peasant's fantasy. Because of this proclivity, their histories became thoroughly confusing. This didn't seem to concern them though. Rather, to signify the passing of generations, and the ongoing procession of their own lives, the longest-lived ones would shed names like trees dropping leaves in the fall. Thus, allowing one set of life images to fade as another cycle of friends and acquaintances disappeared into their own winters. Very much like changing robes. As life seasons transited into new springs, entirely new cycles of friends, acquaintances and adversaries emerged, with yet another round of dealings and reckonings. Lu Shang freely admitted having worn other names in the past, but they didn't matter. "Lu Shang would be fine from here on out. Or if you like the thought of the hermit fisherman, call me Jiang Ziya."

And so, it was.

He also recalled how King Di had never once asked his name. "In my years of service in Shang, then even when confined, it had always been 'you,' or 'old man,' or even 'the lunatic.' Like all others in that kingdom, I existed simply for exploitation. Names meant nothing to the royal pair; they let their servants worry about those things. You filled a purpose, then became disposable. Calling you by a name or otherwise recognizing your identity dissipated royal essence."

History knows him formally as Jiang Ziya, a strategist whose prominence has spanned the ages. Respecting the judgment of history, we shall also know him by that name from this point.

Soon after returning to the palace, King Wen surprised the court yet again, proclaiming the sage to be his new Prime Minister. No one lost their job or position. Until then, Zhou had no Prime Minister. This signaled for all something new, and different. As newly declared first among the ministers, he not only had the King's constant ear, but also his trust. In that new post, he gained firm footing within Wen's authority of state. From that point, the pair seemed almost connected at the hip, side by side, rarely apart.

When this happened, some felt slighted at the inexplicable ascension of an unknown, let alone an outsider, to what would become the most influential post in the land. Before long, even the doubters and naysayers had to concede and credit the old man's obvious brilliance, once witnessed unbridled. Besides, he had a considerate leaning in how he approached the delicate matters of propriety, feelings, status, and might we add, ego. He never resisted, or impeded, or insinuated, or belittled. The common observation trickled out that whoever he interfaced with seemed to get much better at whatever it was they did; though no one could remember him ever telling them to do anything differently, or in any other way not already of their own choosing. Rather than seeing him to be a foe or competitor for influence, the King's collection of ministers soon vied for the sage's attention, clinging to his every word as an opportunity to peer into the workings of his great mind. He possessed an undeniable grasp of the Tao, which through him showered its benign influence abundantly on all he did, most particularly, his stratagems and inter-faces. Simply knowing him, one felt exalted.

The evil Di Xin clearly missed the boat on this. That error would prove costly.

With his sage now in hand, as had been long foretold, King Wen now pressed Jiang Ziya to develop a war strategy. One which would enable Zhou to move against the much larger Shang, and to end the misery of its people while assuring Zhou's own safety and independence.

Jiang Ziya flat out refused to do so. He remained steadfast on this, no doubt stretching the very bounds of his nascent relationship with his newfound benefactor. As you might suspect, associations like this often proved quite tenuous. No one understood this better than Jiang Ziya. Why would it be any different here? He had been down that road before. But not so far down the road that he would give less than sagely counsel to his new friend, or less than the truth. "You can't cut off the head of Shang and expect to solve your problems, or their problems. It can never be that way. In careless warfare, there are no winners. If you defeat Shang, what plans do you have for the day following, the month following, the year following? You have no plans of course; no one ever does. Defeat Di Xin and where does that leave you? With a hornet's nest in your hands, as you shout 'Victory!' Such victories are short lived, while the costs are long." He counseled patience, stressing how in the present moment Zhou remained a land with vast potential, not yet nearly realized. "Better first to grow one's base to where the root stands impregnable and unshakable. Right here is where greatest opportunity lies. Seek victory here first, right under your nose." Often, he reminded, "Time favors Zhou; and like water, erodes the foundation of Shang from within. This happens even as you look the other way, and seemingly do nothing but pick your nose. In this affair, patience must rule."

The Six Secret Teachings

Once he got past his disappointment, King Wen took Jiang's words to heart. "The old buzzard might piss me off at times, but dammit, has he ever been wrong about anything?" What the sage chose not to say spoke the loudest. A defeat of Di Xin would likely mark the end of Shang, as no one there had the stature or influence to step into his vacant shoes. The vacuum would result in disintegration of the Shang state, and from the pieces remaining, new factions would in time coalesce. First into roving bands, then into brigand armies, eventually melded into legions under the control of warlords looking to claim domains of their own. Prosperous Zhou would beckon them like a ripened fruit, existing only to appease their quenchless appetites. Really, a situation no different than today's.

Though Jiang Ziya had discreetly avoided the topic, it would fall to whoever conquered Shang to establish a new dynasty in its place. A decrepit and dissipated empire would eventually fall, and from its ashes, renewal and perhaps change for the better would come in the form of another. Long united, must divide; long divided, must unite.[20] A riddle wrapped inescapably within the Tao. Old Jiang had lived and experienced enough to see how far to the right or wrong, the attitudes of men forever drove the wheels of

---

[20] Riddle of fate and destiny memorialized in the Classic of The Three Kingdoms

change. It seemed to be a rule as certain as the seasons and as the day trading places with the night. Whatever, which men held most tightly, seemed eventually to be inadequate to the dictates of their needs and their ambitions. Thus, the engine of change rolled continuously along. Grinding the present into the future.

The more powerful you were, the more vulnerable you became. Kings, above all, seemed powerless to do anything about it. But it didn't keep them from trying. They clung and held, then looked for more of what they clung to, never quite apprehending how clinging itself ensured all would in time come loose and lost; gone from their grip. Only the fragments remained. Pickings hoarded and re-assembled by the next in line.

Only on the cusps of these events might one find true brilliance or decadence. Each at its most potent, one seemingly unable to exist without the other, or perhaps creating the other. Could that be what best explained the "Why?" of Di Xin. Or the just emergence, against incredibly significant odds mind you, of Ji Chang. True, the Tao embraced all and stood essentially unaffected by the affairs of men. Acting apart, upholding dharma, assuring always its virtue would prevail. All King Wen could do at this point would be to ensure the form, character, and inclination of whatever came in Shang's place. Trusting, as had been the case with every new cycle, the hopes of humankind would renew, and there would be yet another chance to circumvent folly. Wise King Wen would prepare his world for the future, and then hope for the best.

For his part, Minister Jiang counseled how Zhou stood as a cup, now barely one-quarter filled to its potential. It befell King Wen to bring it to full measure. Only then would Zhou be able to deal with Shang as an equal; and by that, avoid its own untimely end.

Though disappointed he would not have his long-sought revenge on Di Xin, at least not right away, Wen agreed on the need to bring Zhou to full realization. *"Better to be a beacon shining bright promise through the torments of chaos, than to be a cat clawing uselessly on a despot's back."*

So, with the sage at his side, he gradually became the King against whom all others would be measured and compared over time.

The emerging Zhou became a model for the ages. Rightfully governed by a just and caring monarch, fostered by a sage who counseled a country would become powerful only to the extent the people within prospered. "Let love and compassion guide your decisions. Then study how the mysterious acts on its own. Resonating to what you have set in motion, filling all cups, contenting all stomachs, and freeing the population to actualize their true nature. Then, make sure to stay the hell out of the way."

In some disangled ways, Jiang Ziya owed his own burden of debt to Shang's royal couple for what he managed to glean from their sordid example. Over the course of his five hundred years, he had seen some terrible reigns. But not a single one had been so base and dysfunctional as that of Di Xin and his cohort, the witch Daji. Jiang had always been a learned man, a sage in fact. Long before first encountering the roving ministers of Shang. With his foresight and his clever quickness, he had always in the past adroitly managed to skirt evil's many dung heaps. Not so when he met up with Di Xin and Daji. With them, he stumbled awkwardly and unknowing. Out of his element, backing himself directly into the center of their storm.

In recounting to King Wen, he never spoke harshly of his confinement; explaining only, "I made a terrible mistake; and I paid the dreadful price." Likewise for his long and tortuous charade of madness, "I did it to save my skin; my skills at pretense proved convincing. Had they not, I'd surely be dead already. Even for that, and the suffering, I have no regrets. It brought me deeper within myself than I had ever imagined possible; opening new doors of awareness upon which I have now grown to fully rely. Little escapes my notice these days." Having spent the time he did under their watchful scrutiny, he managed from their perverse example to perfect his art of leadership in accordance with the Tao. He accomplished this by witnessing firsthand all which they did, and recognizing the Tao lay in doing the precise opposite.

In a shorter time than one would think, the two friends grew closer than had they been blood relations. Is it not fortunate how we can choose who in life we will ultimately depend on? With our relations and siblings, it is not so easy. Blood ties tend to muddle our thoughts and judgments. But seeing talent in a stranger, one can act cleanly and decisively. In the end, the bond of complete trust proves stronger and thicker than any tie of blood.

That's how it became with them. Often, when together, one might start to say something, and the other would finish the thought, carefully polishing it to a finer sheen. Together they strove as one to raise Zhou to prosperity and its people to their full measure. This proved no slight task, and the effort spanned many years. During that period, scholarship grew and then thrived, as did philosophy and the arts, particularly poetry, for which the period is especially renowned. These same hallmarks of culture had long become stagnant and putrid in Shang.

At King Wen's encouragement, and finally, insistence, Jiang Ziya systematically formalized the essence of his life lessons. At the King's behest, he memorialized them into his classic treatise on strategy, known to history as *The Six Secret Teachings*[21]. As the first to read it, King Wen instantly recognized it to be a timeless masterpiece. He decreed it a state-wide requirement of study for all who aspired to higher positions and levels of trust within Zhou. Why, even the foot soldiers committed its precepts to memory; using the sound principles to guide their own involvements with those they served and those they opposed.

Within the narrative, Jiang Ziya preserves for all time the very marrow of his hard gleaned wisdom. It represents a crowning monument to his struggle, and re-emergence. Not a word wasted, not a word left out. You may not know what you need to know, but likely will find it there. Within, he emphasizes the value of talent and relationships, permeated with trust, yielding no harbor to suspicions and fear. He speaks intently on the tactics of warfare and the development of state and infrastructure as well as actions and counters apropos in every situation. All the while emphasizing conquering through righteousness; and wherever possible, without need for a single battle or the purposeless shedding of blood. He set forth his Dragon Strategy, the creation of a functional command within a viable strategic hierarchy without which there would be no prospect for surviving an onslaught from Shang. The Tiger, Leopard and Dog Strategies provided clear maps into the constellations of tactical possibilities leaving nothing

---

[21] "T'ai Kung's Six Secret Teachings". Trans. Ralph D. Sawyer. In Sawyer, Ralph D., *The Seven Military Classics of Ancient China*. New York: Basic Books. 2007. p. 40.

unaddressed in the proper comportment of a strategic force having no alternative but to enter direct engagement.

For once, relying on a long lifetime of hard scraped lessons, many at great personal cost, he left no stone unturned in accounting for all eventualities. Looking to future dealings with Shang, engaging those same principles, the formula clarified to this—King Di and the witch would have no escape. Only the matter of proper timing remained; and therein would lay the prospects for success; or a dismal failure which would consume all.

Death by a Thousand Cuts

Only after his own close study of the *Secret Teachings* did King Wen fully comprehend the vulnerability of Zhou, positioned next to the Shang colossus. It troubled him in no small measure that he had been looking selflessly, or so he thought, and with the best of intentions to rid Shang of its plague. His acting on such high-minded inclinations would have spelled ruin. Timing is the emperor of change. Prepare meticulously, then act. Jiang's treatise made all so clear. Wen had failed to recognize his own inadequacy to accomplish the objective; or the consequences which would befall both Zhou and Shang should he fail.

Well, he knew now. Restraint. He would chance nothing. Step forward only when the root stands firm, and independent. When the time came, they would bank their destiny on a more certain victory. Nothing less would suffice. There could be no fall back or alternate course contemplated in the grand plan whenever it took its final shape.

Often, in the early mornings, the King frequented the temples, making offerings and giving thanks. Destiny had spared him from the blunder of a premature campaign. Now, with renewed clarity of purpose, he dedicated his energies and immense talents to the betterment of Zhou. Preparing it for the future and the unknown, whatever it might encompass. There could be no doubt, the final solution to Shang's woes would be a prosperous and

powerful Zhou. No other players out there fit the bill. As he
readied the game board for the final play, he recognized
with no small regret the day of judgment for Shang would
not come from his hand. He had aged much faster than his
preparations yielded their fruit. Though he prayed and
made constant offerings petitioning the task fall to him
during his reign, it had become clear. It simply could not be.
Already the sharp teeth of time nipped harshly at his tunic,
sure to latch tightly before the hoped for opportunity arose.
So, for that eventual task, he prepared his second son, who
would in time come to succeed him as King Wu.

Why, even his name meant "martial."

No doubt, you wonder *Why not groom the first son to this
purpose.* Sadly, I must tell you.

You see, not for an instant did King Wen and his
emerging Zhou escape the notice of the diabolical Daji. Like
a jealous goddess with heads scouring all directions, her
ever alert eyes soon inclined their focus on Zhou's
ascendance. *"It makes no sense. Why aren't they like us? What
could they possibly be up to?"* She and Di Xin knew King Wen
had grown too old to bear the responsibilities and rigors of a
major campaign against Shang. In that, they felt secure.
Initially, their spies confirmed Zhou's armed forces to be
weak, and possessing no taste for battle let alone prolonged
engagement. They'd be no match for the forces of Shang.
Their troops had been in constant deployment spanning
decades.

Shang's armies faced endless trials and campaigns. When
not quelling unrest along the frontiers, securing the borders,
or purging opposition, they were knocking down rebellions
sprouting about them like weeds. You would think demands
like this would have devastated their morale. Not so. Fact is,
what Shang officer would not prefer the rigors of isolation

and combat to the unending suspicion and scrutiny, let alone abuse, should they ever find themselves too near the court and within the purview of the feared and despised royal twosome. On the field of battle, one at least had the soldier's fighting chance to survive another day. Lamentable prospects bettering the alternatives. So much for motivation.

Shang, as you've probably gathered, had fallen prey to its own fears. Hasn't this always been the case with empires? And hasn't it always proven true that in their doing so, reality responded by shifting over time to justify them? So, the reasons for your fears soon enough became your future. And in that, Tao assures never ending change, the ultimate underpinning of all hope for the future.

So, Shang kept its wary eye on Zhou. For Zhou, before the ascension of Jiang Ziya, the state infrastructure could not have supported a major campaign. Supply lines would have been woefully inadequate for any projection of force beyond their borders. It had been a fact. Apart from King Wen, and his first son Bo Yikao, Zhou had no leaders or generals with the requisite stature or charisma to sustain a substantive challenge against Shang. Knowing this, the ministers of Shang remained satisfied, deploying resources elsewhere, while carefully mining the tenuous detente between the kingdoms. They viewed Zhou as Shang's rural outback, and not a realm of comparable stature or significance. A bunch of hicks, actually. Still, Shang strategists watched with interest, perhaps envy. Over the years, under King Wen's careful stewardship, Zhou prospered and grew. Shang stagnated and depleted itself on exhausting campaigns quelling troublesome neighbors, enemies within, or barbarians from afar. Not to mention the wild and undisciplined splurges of Di Xin in his ever-expanding efforts to appease the visions and demands of Daji. Their lakes of wine, and forests of meats and sweets; the frequent scenes of orgies involving thousands of likeminded adherents, all swearing eternal loyalty and service to whatever the two might beckon. Does it not amaze? How many odd and different currents run within the streams of time?

Now, for reasons all too obvious, Zhou captured the interest of the royal couple. Possibly even before their ministers, and their strategists, the royal couple saw how Zhou appeared to have turned the critical corner. No longer a rural outback, somehow becoming the beneficiary of unseen blessings in the form of a guiding spirit who could seemingly do no wrong. Might that have been this Jiang Ziya? Some time ago, their spies told them of a new minister. An old man who seemingly walked out of the wilderness directly into his appointment by King Wen as first among ministers. Why had they not heard this name before? Who was he? Where did he come from?

Even now, still brilliant in her skill at sensing and assessing threats, Daji noted the changes in Zhou, and reckoned a time would come when she, along with the King's personal assassins would of necessity secretly visit the Zhou palace with the Assassin's Mace and render Zhou once again to its rightful insignificance. But not quite yet. For the time being, Zhou filled a vital role. It remained a tenuous vassal whose very presence insulated Shang from even more imminent threats from the outlying warring kingdoms. Zhou served as Shang's buffer, freeing Shang to maintain forces along the Northern and Eastern frontiers, where they were most needed. *"It had become all so complicated."* Though she sensed no imminent threat from King Wen, he was after all an old man; the jaundiced heart of Daji took careful measure of all other possibilities and lit her interest upon his first son Bo Yikao[22]. Or it might simply have been his good looks. In him, she found one who bore the same traits of character and stoutness of heart as his father, as well as having youth, stamina, and great charisma. Clearly, a threat. As she admired him from afar, her thoughts went to her own Di Xin, who until her first sight of Bo Yikao, had stood alone as most perfect among all men.

And for that, Bo Yikao paid a terrible price. At Daji's insistence, and to ensure Zhou's continued loyalty, Di Xin, yielding to his wife's endless pleading, summoned Bo Yikao to be Zhou's emissary to the Shang throne. In short, a royal hostage.

The full particulars of his fate languish beneath the blanket of history. One day King Wen received a communique from King Di advising with empathy, sadness and regret how noble Prince Bo Yikao had stolen off with one of the royal concubines. Di Xin reminded how tradition dictated the penalty for such offense to be death and dishonor, though he had restrained his hand, respecting the great affection he held for King Wen. With tacit restraint, he allowed Bo Yikao the privilege to act on his own behalf, expecting the Prince would take his own life and that of the concubine, rather than bring dishonor to Zhou. Instead, the lad, perhaps from immaturity, perhaps selfishness, or worse, ignored the freely granted chance to preserve honor. Preferring to save his own hide, he disappeared without a trace, taking the young lady with him into the western wilderness. Di Xin felt the Prince would never again dare to show his face either in Shang, or in Zhou, and as far as that went, we should add no fuel to the embarrassing affair.

---

[22] First son of King Wen of Zhou (Ji Chang); elder brother to King Wu. Believed to have pre-deceased his father.

"Certainly, nothing for us to war over; simply water under life's bridge, never seen again. We must both live with this tragic loss and find the will to move on." While Di Xin purportedly mourned the loss of a favored concubine, he reminded of his confidence the honorable Ji Chang would make right and compensate the loss, which he agreed for all time to keep only between the two of them.

King Wen saw through the perfidious lie of course and knew his son had joined their honorable ancestors. Saying nothing further on this, he issued a royal decree designating Prince Wu as his eventual successor. The population of Zhou knew only they had a new crown prince and suspicioned precisely what this meant. It could be only one thing. To a person, from oldest to youngest, native born or struggling immigrant, each swore eternal oaths of loyalty to their beloved surviving Prince and their King.

It took some years. In the learning, he never found the heart to directly tell his people. King Wen and his Prime Minister Jiang Ziya learned from their spies and confidants within Shang how, in the matter of Bo Yikao, Daji had outdone herself. In ancient times, there came into common use an expression conveying the sense of great suffering, "Death by a Thousand Cuts." We say no more than that.

Discretion aside, as time passed, the unmentionable atrocity became common knowledge to all. The account seemed to have grown wings of its own, born by rumor's swift currents to all corners of the great land. Even the barbarians to the North, the South and East spoke of it with horror and disbelief, their empathy falling squarely to King Wen and Zhou.

So, the stage had been set. Ji Chang and Jiang Ziya dedicated their remaining time together to the prime objective. Actualize Zhou and its people, secure all outlying areas, assimilate the lessor vassal states and stand ever ready to act. Build loyalties, inform, educate, encourage, share, and reward. As to the nobility, intermarry, create blood ties with all and delegate. In the end, Zhou became what chroniclers described as a family state, functioning as a familial extension of the royal household. By the time Ji Chang's reign drew to its close, Zhou solidified into a formidable nation. No longer anyone's outback. They prospered beyond all prior measure.

Old Friends Reminisce

As the King eventually aged and deteriorated, his long-trusted friend and mentor Jiang Ziya seemed ever to be the still spry seventy-two-year-old he first encountered fishing by the stream. As he entered his ninety sixth year, Wen's affection for his friend had not diminished in any way. That, despite their sometimes-frothy disagreements on minuscule points of philosophy, strategy or administration. Judging by what the old King had witnessed and determined for himself, he had long ago concluded Master Jiang to have been an ageless river spirit; perhaps even a dragon residing in the borrowed form of a man. Sometimes the old King would grudgingly mumble, "Better yet he be a dragon, since that best suited his celestial nature."

Not until facing his final days did old Ji Chang beg to question his friend regarding how he cleverly managed to cheat the effects of time. He reminded Master Jiang how there had been a day not too long ago when Jiang Ziya had been the elder, and Wen the younger. At least judging by all outward appearances. It defied logic how he now stared grimly at death's fast widening door, while his friend went about his affairs the same as he had always done since the day they first met. How many years ago was that? One loses track.

But for this single divergence, they had in many ways become one, and would have remained so indefinitely. But then again there stood the dictates of nature, to which even great monarchs must humbly submit.

Jiang Ziya, realizing his friend's end to be fast approaching, answered candidly, telling of how he had once sought immortality. "I had even made inroads, perfecting some of its subtle nuances, but not so well as to arrest all the effects of aging." Old Wen wanted to know everything. He didn't mean the secrets of immortality. What good would that do him at this point? He wanted to hear all about Jiang's long tenure. The full recount of a direct eyewitness to history, and not some twisted history conjured up by court scholars seeking favor with some ego driven monarch. What all had Jiang done? What had he seen? Where had he been? What were his impressions? Did he encounter any genuinely great men? Sages? Seers? Dragons? What about the stars? Did his long view give him better vantage to their mysteries and influences?

Jiang had never spoken of these things to anyone in recent generations. *"Best to let past events rest"* had been his thought. But this moment stood above all the others. Yes, he had met great men, but to this point, and by his reckoning, none could match the greatness of the man here beside him. Wanting to hold nothing back from his esteemed friend, the great sage sat alongside old Wen for the next several days. He faithfully shared the stories, adventures, details and discoveries of his long personal history. A history spanning over five centuries. Notably, he made sure to include his torment at the hands of Di Xin and Daji, recounting the tragedy of his escape. He wept over the lives uselessly lost, his personal burden of responsibility, as well as the regrets over his errors in judgment. "I never should have gone to the palace, and I never should have sealed the borders when acting as Prime Minister. Silly old fool I was, thinking I could somehow redeem Di Xin. If one wishes to describe how far a noble soul can fall, he need only say two words 'Di Xin.' Everyone will know the meaning. For me, they mean 'Lost without hope.' Even when he prayed, fulfilling his responsibilities as monarch. His time at the royal temple seemed to damn him all the more. I saw with my own eyes. Dark shadows ominously enveloped his prostrate figure. Sacred images seeming to turn their gazes away. For those witnessing these alarming portents, one irrefutable conclusion emerged. No act of man or spirit could undo Di Xin's deviation from righteousness. There could be no return to his birth nature, now forever forfeit."

As to the sage's own remorse, old King Wen would hear none of Jiang's regrets over his failures and miscalculations, insisting only, "You came to me as the finished diamond, brilliant in all its aspects. Soundly forged and shaped by an imperfect past. You should have no misgivings. We cannot control all those events and influences which make us into who we become. Life's currents do not dance to our call, we can only aim our own fragile vessel to where we choose. In that you acted impeccably. Before you judge yourself harshly, look today where it has taken you. No other men could have accomplished what you and I have in our time together. Only the course you took long before we met brought us here. Together! I am content to let history judge us, on the balance of what we return to it. I for one am satisfied.

"Never allow yourself to forget. Without you, certain ruin would have befallen Zhou. Even on the fateful hunt where we first met, I had already been planning for the imminent invasion of Shang. No longer would I be content to bide my time, having to bear disturbed witness to the never-ending stream of atrocities. Speaking of your judgment upon yourself, how would you have regarded my miscalculations had I done that?

"Only you, having learned what you did from your past and your time with Di Xin. Only you managed to convince and restrain me when I was gnawing at the bit to attack Shang and liberate its people. Liberate Shang! At least that's how I tried to justify it to myself. But in my heart, thoughts of vengeance boiled over like a cauldron of poison, clouding my reason. Without you, I would not have seen any of this clearly. Let there be no confusion, our coming together was destined. That's my own assessment. To this day I make daily offerings at the temple. I leave no doubt as to my gratitude to the heavens for turning you into a terrible fisherman, and drawing your plight to my fancy as I happened by one blessed day. Think about it. If anything had been different, we would never even have met! How disastrous would my attacking Shang have been? Only you stayed my hand and my sword. No one else could have done that. You would do well to start each day asking yourself these questions. 'What if we had never met? What if I had not stayed Wen's hand? What would have become of our world?'

Jiang Ziya, now thinking of Bo Yikao, answered his friend. "One thing I've learned over my many years. In the end, we never truly know if the actions we take will produce the results we intend. I have learned, however, the importance of striving impeccably, accounting for all possibilities, and opting first for harmony and restraint if that's where they point. Restraint, along with proper and nuanced timing of one's actions, gives incalculable advantage, and leverage.

A move on Shang when you first proposed would have been ill-timed. You had not placed the groundwork necessary for success, a tree with underdeveloped roots cannot weather a strong wind, let alone a great and treacherous typhoon. The witch Daji, a brilliant strategist as you well know, would surely have banked on this. Perhaps even to the point of enticing the attack and gleaning the advantages of leverage for her own forces.

At that point, timing favored the Shang. They didn't act because other more pressing contingencies drew their attention and their energy. Zhou might have lost all, and the scourge of Shang would have poured like a great tidal wave from within the confines of its borders. Still, who can say for certain what would have happened? These thoughts merely represent my calculations. No more no less. And who am I besides a very, very old fool. I have witnessed fate smiling on the ill prepared. For them, even elephants will dance on the heads of pins. No one can predict for certain if and when this will occur. Would fate have blessed your impatience, or your audacity? Who knows this, or anything, for certain? We have only ourselves, our insights into the way, and our trust in its oneness and its rightness. After five hundred years, I bring nothing more to the table. Anything else would cloud reality and tempt absurdity. While what you say may be true. That in our restraint we managed to avoid catastrophe. Still, even now, I am convinced of absolutely nothing except this. The price of our choice proved dear beyond measure; by foregoing invasion, we set into motion events which resulted in the loss of our beloved Prince Bo Yikao, the embodiment of our dreams for all we hoped Zhou would become. With that, they thought to have removed our head. Instead, they steeled our resolve. But the price. Oh, the price!"

Old King Wen could not bear to think of his first son, and his flagrant murder at the hands of Daji. The single reprieve being his certainty the orb had not consumed his soul. Jiang Ziya had long before made his new sovereign aware of all he knew regarding the dreaded device. The sage felt its use against competing sovereigns and rising princes to be inescapable. He told of how Di Xin and Daji had hoped to make it a battlefield weapon. But clearly, its greatest utility lay in its stealthiness, and the finality of its touch, an assassin's tool supreme. When first hearing of the Prince's disappearance, they feared above all that noble Bo Yikao had fallen prisoner to the mace, cast adrift in eternity. Strange, isn't it? How things can be. Learning of his death by a thousand cuts both heightened and lessened their despair.

Doubtless this is why, as his sunset drew inevitably closer, Ji Chang summoned Prince Wu to his chamber. On entering, the Prince saw his father and Jiang Ziya, whom he loved almost as a father, and considered to be an esteemed uncle. He found them together, inseparable, as he had always known them to be.

Seeing him enter, Wen called him forward, reminding as he always took care to do, "When the time comes, I ask only you remember your brother Bo Yikao as you cleanse the detritus of Shang from the face of our great land. Purge their ashes, leave no trace, take no chances, and no matter what they offer in return, give no quarter to the royal couple. Show them how we reciprocate their unwanted favors once extended to your noble brother."

From earliest childhood, both his father and his uncle had groomed Prince Wu for this daunting task. As they had with Bo Yikao, the King and his sage companion spared no effort cultivating the young and surviving Prince for the role destiny had bequeathed to him. They had every confidence in him—he had in all respects become his brother's equal.

In truth, he needed no reminders. The child Wu, on first learning the circumstances of his brother's end, took a blade and inscribed the characters for his brother's name into his left forearm. On entering his bed chamber, the shocked father discovered the boy warrior painted in red, staring intently at his work. Speechless, Wen approached the child, already losing consciousness from the loss of blood. The boy looked up, aware only enough to say, "We must never forget Bo Yikao, father." At those words, King Wen reached his arm around the boy's shoulders and sat quietly alongside. In his embrace he stared intently at the wound, then gripped tightly with his free hand, quelling the flow of blood.

"No son, we will never forget."

Giving Voice to Final Doubts

Prince Wu would undoubtedly remember Bo Yikao to the royal couple when he came to pay final respects. He dedicated his life to that end. Trained by the masters in his youth, the most diligent pupil. Never tiring, he worked his sword each day, dawn to dusk. With every reach for the scabbard, he saw his brother's name engraved in flesh, just as he drew the blade. One thought always tied to the other. Years later, with the court in session, others noted how he bared his sleeve, seeming to recite a wordless mantra.

"The evil two will receive no quarter from me when my time comes."

King Wen reached for his son, and as they embraced, he surreptitiously lifted the short blade from the Prince's belt. Then he turned to Jiang Ziya, "Tell me Brother Jiang. Speak truthfully now. How much time do you have remaining?"

The elder stood pensive, focused as though calculating, then could only shrug his shoulders. "It stands uncertain sire. The ability to stall time diminishes as one ages. Now the years fly by so quickly. Ofttimes, it seems my incline toward prolonging the effort has lessened. Only to you two do I confess. These days, it seems the energy demanded by the deed depletes me no less than nature itself."

Prince Wu did not yet know or share the full scope of the sage's secret, nor did he know now of what they spoke. Despite this, he could readily see the gravity of the sage's saddened demeanor as he stood and hovered over the diminishing Wen, once his King, now his beloved friend.

Looking at them, the Prince thought, *"What would the old sage do without father? The two, so perfectly wound together. His yin to father's yang. Could one even remain without the other's binding influence? Perhaps they plan to leave together ..."* Did that explain the knife in King Wen's grip? In those times, such sacrifice between friends would not have been uncommon. More so should the friend be a wife, servant, or concubine.

But Jiang Ziya had much remaining on his slate of things to do. The steeled gaze of the two men locked tight. Both knew the call of duty, and the importance of their roles.

The King struggled against his tired and aching bones a bit, then carefully pulled himself upright where he could see better into the eyes of his friend. "Where we stand today has come at great cost to myself and my family. Still, I have no regrets. As hell frothed all about us, our once insignificant State of Zhou prospered and grew strong. Never before in history has a state so loosened the shackles of ignorance and bondage. Chains which had for so long bound its people to servitude, deprivation and suffering.

This concerted effort spanned several generations of my people, starting with my noble grandfather Danfu. As a formidable warrior chieftain, he detested the waste and tragedy of conflict. Duke Danfu strove for partnership, loyalty, mutual respect, and support. Guided always by justice and humanity. He carefully modeled those traits for his followers; knowing how Tao preferred to imprint more than to conquer, always evolving toward its ever-renewing state. He would frequently prompt, 'Never forget, child. The Tao roots in peace. Without peace, where can one find freedom? Without freedom, why go on?'

"Fleeing from endless discord, his tribe of one-time cave dwellers ultimately found their sanctuary in the Wei River Basin. Just as foretold to him by repeated casts of the oracle bones. For our tribe, the remote Wei became a safe haven. A refuge beyond oppression's reach. As you well know, skilled in the ancient arts of reading portents, Danfu even predicted our own eventual meeting. Now, I, his grandson, prepare to join him in the celestial retreat. Our state of Zhou has grown robust, fully formed and viable. Plentiful resources abound. We have commerce and trade with all corners of the land. There exists peace and harmony everywhere within our borders. And we've built a strong army, grounded soundly upon your six principles. Our infrastructure can confidently bear the weight of our intentions, wherever they may lead or take us. As my grandfather would have wished of us, even as we grew and prospered, we looked about for those in need of our help and support, always extending a compassionate hand. Even at times granting passage to entire populations of the oppressed Shang. Allowing safety within our own borders. Many amongst us disagreed, some even argued against. Daunting challenges lined before us, necessitating great sacrifice on our parts, as well as boundless tolerance for change and uncertainty.

"I delighted when you reminded those opposing how we were no different in our own first coming to this land. Oppressed, destitute and forlorn, taking refuge here because anything bettered from whence we came. As you know, it turned out our own concerns over those who followed proved unfounded. The forecasted burden of the new ones showed soon enough to be a blessing. In less than a generation they became one with our people, so disgusted had they become with the decadence of their once homeland. Can there be any doubt where they saw their future? Our future? Even with nothing else gained from this point, history will read our sacrifices as achievements on our part, serving to counter and offset the leanings of a world tilting hard toward madness. They will stand like fine calligraphy scrolled onto history. Signifying our aspirations for all to bear witness. Proving our standards of decency possessed real bite, capable of sinking teeth into action when called to do so.

"Still, the times remain afflicted and pitted with danger. We endure. Ever mindful a great threat still looms. So close, I can already smell the brimstone. Surely you can too Brother Jiang. It draws near like a panther stalking in the darkness, even as we speak. As you already know, we prevailed over Shang's efforts to weaken us, and even to eliminate us. The price for my clan has been great, almost too great to bear. I will say this again. But for your wise counsel and oft steadying influence, better men than I would have succumbed to the base inclinations. Strike first, figure later. I have lost friends, uncles and cousins, as well as a noble father and a son to their treachery and deceit. Were it not for the stintless sacrifice of my nobles, I too would have shared their same fate. Yet, in spite of it all, the great costs, the loss and sacrifice, we have become something better, even unique in the record of time. Like a Phoenix, we continually rose from our own ashes, stronger and more formidable than before. By seeking to grind us back to the stone age, our adversary left us no alternative but to grow complete, and thus forged the keys to its own undoing. In Zhou, we have a once insignificant family clan, now grown into the hard and noble reality of a formidable kingdom. A kindly web embracing all. Within Zhou, I am the father, they, the children; I am the brother, they, the siblings; I am the husband, they the spouse. We stand in communal union, where each of us supports the other. Where all can work together for and perhaps to even achieve, their highest aspirations."

He stared deep into the soul of his ancient friend. "And yet, I fear to the very core of my marrow. What if we have not prepared adequately? Where might we have erred? Have we overlooked something? A vulnerability? Or perhaps we have deluded ourselves. Forgetting through our own carelessness. It is Shang and not Zhou which possesses the mandate of heaven? Haven't they said their royal line descended from Shangdi, chief of the gods? Can we be so arrogant and self-possessed to think Shang will fall simply because we have made so meticulously ready, or because we hope or want them to? I fear that corpses of others not so unlike us at all litter the trail of history. Even now, as we gather today, Prince Wu doubtless attracts the wary eye of Daji. There can be no illusions where that will lead. Make no mistake on this, she will strike soon, particularly as I weaken over the coming months, weeks, and then days. Would that I could have shared the full tread of your time, old man. There's no telling what we might have accomplished, and what ill renderings of destiny might have avoided."

The sage nodded and half-smiled solemnly in acknowledgment. "Yes Brother Ji, we have made a fine pair during our brief time together. All too short, given our hopes and our yearnings. You don't know this, but I first came to the Wei River wilderness to recover. I arrived as a ghost of my former self, infected and torn asunder by the leprous touch of Di Xin and his evil consort Daji. My spirit had grown dismally ill and forlorn, my will to do anything blighted. No different than anyone else in their domain. All the disciplines, all the studies, the philosophies, the break throughs, the failures, successes and lessons learned … then in the end, when pitted against the final task of defeating true evil, of no consequence. Except to further advance the perverted ambitions of the two most sinister beings ever to cross my weary and so earnestly trodden path. Escaping with my life, but only my life, all else ripped from my being and laid to waste. As had been so with the many others, who fared far worse. I sought the comfort and refuge of isolation, and craved silence. My remedy, a place free of screams. There I waited, as I fished without purpose, for kind death to show its hand. Immortality be damned! Only one thought buoyed my hopes. Karma, and the possibility greater awarenesses than mine would have a play in this game.

"I will tell you this. It is not so easy to explain, but perhaps both of you will understand. Over my long years, many spent as an astute student and observer of the flows of destiny coursing through the affairs of humankind; I searched for meaningful threads, patterns if you will. It seemed almost possible at times to come to grips with them. Even to some limited but discernible degree, to comprehend them. Certainly, they remained tightly cloaked in mystery, but what constitutes mystery to a single lifetime; becomes more readily familiar when viewed through the prism of ten lifetimes. While hard answers continued to elude, one particular phenomenon emerged to my awareness. So certain its presence, one might count it as a universal law, like the cycles of the moon and the stars. Or perhaps the trickling finger of Karma, or even the tactile emergence of Dharma bubbling through life's undulating moments. Sometimes it's subtle, so much so, you can easily miss it or mistake it. What triggers it, you see, is when someone does grievous wrong to another.

"We all have our own thoughts as to whether our actions cast their long shadows, birthing counterparts in the scales of merit, reward, justice and retribution. The teachings of the ancients struggle to address this. But who's to say what they know or don't know. Belief can be its own reward. Becoming its own reality. I have learned not to judge the ancients. But one thing I know as fact. When someone has wronged you and left you alive to simmer in the loss and the injustice. Out there in the deep shadows where Karma's many influences ripple their endless vibrations influencing all which exists, a great wheel slowly begins its turn. On that wheel rests the fates of you the aggrieved and your oppressor, and the past actions which bind you both to the unfathomable rule of Tao. Though I cannot say how, or why, or even where; I can say with absolute belief and certainty that somehow, in some place, and at a precise time which you will recognize when it stands before you, the fate of your once oppressor will rest notched in your sights, with the target of opportunity squared across his breast, waiting only for your finger to move on the release. What happens in that precise moment lies between you and Dharma, and your adversary. Even Di Xin and Daji, with all of their power and evil purpose, will not be spared this certainty, tied so tightly to the accounts of the many they have already wronged."

Wu Ascends
and Waits for a Sign

With a nod of his head, the King signaled his concurrence. He lifted the knife, calling, "Bring your arm here Brother Jiang, I will have you swear our blood oath to see this path through to its only rightful end. We both know in our hearts. The great land will not hold both Zhou and Shang. So long as Shang exists, all we have accomplished stands imminently at risk. One first moment of careless distraction and we become extinct, all of our doings extinguished. The times demand our vigilance. If only to assure our own survival, we must end the scourge of Shang and free its people from their yoke of senseless oppression."

Slowly the old sage reached forward, carefully taking the blade from his friend. He then turned and extended it respectfully. Handing it forward with both hands to the Prince, who took it and held it steady, not knowing for sure what was expected of him.

Jiang Ziya turned back to face Ji Chang. "We both know what remains Brother Ji. We both know the weight of history weighing upon us. We both know what will happen if we fail. If we do not carve our mark on the walls of time, no one will know we were ever here. There will be no second chances for the likes of us. The slow turning table yet turns as we speak today. Karma yearns to soon settle its long open accounts with the evil ones. You have my oath; I will see this through." Turning to Prince Wu, he continued, "When the time is right, we together will pull the bow string and loose the arrow. The legacy of Di Xin and Daji will fall. Dropping down and deep like a carcass riddled with the weight of its own evil deeds, consumed and forgotten in the seas of time."

The glare of steel in Wu's eyes affirmed without reservation.

Sensing old Wen's look of despondence over his rejection of the blood oath, Jiang Ziya returned to the King. Now cradling the feeble hands of his friend, he spoke, "Sire, you have my word, and my hand on this; there is no better seal. Blood oaths carry no weight here. They are the ceremonies of Shang; a kingdom drenched in blood. In Zhou, we spill no blood needlessly. What I say will be done, I will do. That constitutes the certain measure of our bond. That is who we are!"

Only then did Wen smile his approval, accenting with a thoughtful nod. "Of course, I beg your patience with the insecurity of your suddenly older brother. I find myself having to grapple with this new trait, no doubt rooted in my fast-quickening infirmity."

Given the gravity of the moment, the men simply remained as they were, a fraternity, once of two, now of three. All cognizant of their roles and the weight of their nation's future squared fully on their shoulders.

By the time the day concluded, they had conferenced, analyzed, planned and agreed. Old King Wen would abdicate in favor of his son. Jiang Ziya promised to remain Prime Minister and grand strategist in service to King Wu, swearing only to hold the post until achieving the agreed objective. Anything beyond that, only if requested, serving at the King's request and pleasure. Jiang Ziya knew well enough to get out of the way once finished. The future would belong to King Wu. Jiang would simply fade away, abandoning the stage to others more inclined to its rigors. They had fostered and trained Prince Wu for this task since birth. He too was his father's son, a man of impeccable character.

Though purely serendipitous, their timing, as it turned out, had been exquisite. Rallying to Daji's cries of a rising threat in Zhou, Di Xin had already dispatched his emissaries with orders they return to Shang with Prince Wu. To serve, as had his brother, in the capacity of Zhou's ambassador to the royal court. When the emissaries arrived in Zhou, the recently ascended King Wu peremptorily summoned them to his private chambers. Who knows what he told them? Perhaps that Zhou could spare no more princes to *Death by a Thousand Cuts*? Perhaps that Shang should prepare for its final days—its inevitable end rapidly approached. Whatever he told them, the Shang emissaries left ashen faced to carry his private message back to the royal couple. Judging by the price the emissaries had to pay for returning empty-handed, the royal twosome was no doubt very displeased. The old bronze cylinder glowed red for some time afterward.

In Zhou, King Wen spent his final months away from the court, preferring solitude or the quiet company of Jiang Ziya. He had no wish to distract from, or to interfere with the independence and autonomy of the new King Wu. In some ways, his letting go the long-borne weight of responsibility for his people lightened his heart and freed his time for one of his favorite indulgences. He frequently snuck out to the busy streets of the capital where he drifted aimlessly amidst the common folk. It gave him immense joy to see how freely they moved about, invested in their own purpose. Healthy, clever and industrious; all of it like a vast tapestry where all threads ran independent yet somehow laced together to strengthen the whole. Amazingly, it seemed to run itself. All immersed in the moment, filled with hope with no fear for the future. Yin to Shang's Yang. Not the case in all of Di Xin's crumbling empire, where even infants had to fend for themselves.

Sometimes Jiang Ziya might accompany, both concealing their identities fully delighting in their disguises as old fishermen. Their game typically climaxed with his presenting at the market or some backwater warehouse where, accompanied by his old friend they found sport in haggling with vendors as the two peddled their "catches" and "wares." They took great sport in this, certain of their cleverness, and boasting to each other how they had fooled everyone.

He had always relied on devices like this. What better way to see beneath the cover of the royal household and the palace? In many ways a city-state within a state where all matters seemed ever to be going well, or so his ministers would have had him believe. Perhaps they were indeed going well, but always, he felt compelled to see for himself. *"Feet on the ground, eyes in the crowds, there you will find the true sovereign, intent on learning the state and mind of his people."* His father told him that, just as he in turn had told his own sons. For decades, walking incognito along the common paths and trails, he had come best to learn the ways and fortunes of his people. And in so doing assured for all, but mostly himself, the blessings of the kingdom reached from highest to lowest, which of course, was how it should be. No one did it quite so well before him. Or afterwards, for that matter.

Indeed, would it have surprised the two of them to learn all whom they encountered recognized the two impostors at a glance? So loved by the common folk had they become.

Where on the planet had it ever happened where a market vendor might knowingly argue with his once sovereign, accompanied by the still Prime Minister over the outrageous price set upon a too long ago killed string of carp. And then, unable to strike a bargain, unceremoniously chase them from his stall. For added good measure, and respecting his own investment in the pretense, the vendor might swipe his broom at their bottoms as they scurried away, even he delighting in their obvious mirth, then elderly frustration as they sometimes lost their sandals in the wake.

Yes, laughing like little children they were! It was perhaps as it should be. Wen had always preached to his boys, "The sovereign must be as the sun, ever giving, spreading its light, its joy, and its optimism to all. Ever doing, never faltering, and most importantly, serving as a living example of the way. The people must learn this first by seeing it above, and then attempting, modeling and perfecting it by acting it out within themselves. Rule by doing! Do by leading! Lead first by your own irreproachable example!"

The King and the sage remained inseparable toward the end, ever anticipating that final unavoidable day. You see, nature takes no note of greatness or decrepitude, nor does it stake its reprieve to either. It sees neither as different than you or I see right and left, simply respecting the places where our choices have taken us. It is we and not the Tao or its nature who glean the consequences of what we do. So, for Wen, all his goodness and righteousness purchased not one second more than his allotted ninety-six years. The day would come, of that there could be no doubt. Still, to the tasks he undertook, it proved more than enough.

Elsewhere in the palace, also under the studied eye of his Prime Minister, who at this stage seemed never to sleep,

King Wu made his war plans, formalized alliances, assimilated the weaker states adjoining the periphery of Shang, then bided time. While recognized as a man of his own mind, on one thing, always, he deferred to the wishes of his sage-uncle Jiang Ziya who counseled: "Do not strike until the opportunity fully presents. Not one moment before, not one moment after. All depends on the resonance of this chord being timely struck by your hand. With your impeccable execution, its vibrations will cut to the very core of Shang, reducing it to dust before our sanguine eyes where it shall ever remain, never to rise again."

They all waited, and patiently watched. Now more than anything, looking, even hoping for the opportunity to move. The waiting had begun to take its toll. Nerves became frazzled. Tempers flared inappropriately. All wanted a secure Zhou. All wanted the great threat neutralized. All wanted the sword over their heads cut from its string. King Wen had ruled for forty-nine of his ninety-six years. He had dedicated his life to righteous conduct, the emergence of Zhou, and ultimately, to the fall of Shang. He departed this world as the anticipated day fast neared but did not witness its dawn. At his end, King Wu and Jiang Ziya stood closest by his side. As he took his final breaths, he reached for their hands pulling both close as if to embrace proclaiming, "In the two of you, our future stands bright." And that was it! As he passed, his face froze into a calm smile of contentment, leaving no doubt as to what he saw ahead.

Respecting the final wishes of his father, King Wu took as wife Jiang Yi, the daughter of Jiang Ziya birthed only after his re-emergence and return to new prominence in Zhou. Old as he was, Jiang's new life in Zhou clearly renewed him in more ways than one. Of course, as you might expect, King Wen had a hand in that; relishing the role of matchmaker, pressing until his friend finally relented. Now that Wu had taken Jiang Yi, the two blood lines became in fact as one in the royal offspring who came soon thereafter. They had indeed become a family.

In merging the lines, perhaps wise old Wen had gained the fruit of his blood oath after all.

(To be continued)

A Pact Sealing the Future

Epilogue

I leave these words for my compatriots:

Do not despair.
Though we suffer mistreatment, sorrow and
loss of hope serve no purpose.
Han Xin once endured humiliation yet rose to
be a great general. Foujian faced disgrace before
reclaiming his honor. King Wen, imprisoned at
Youli, would later overthrow King Zhou.
Jiang Taigong endured years of hardship but
was ultimately named a marquis.

Such is the fate of heroes—where great
misfortune breeds the patience necessary
for just retribution.

Excerpt from a poem inscribed on the walls of Angel Island
Immigration Station by an unknown Chinese detainee. This
poem offers solace to fellow detainees, reminding them not
to lose hope despite mistreatment. Drawing parallels to
historical figures who endured hardship before triumphing,
it reflects on resilience, justice, and the strength found in
patience. An elegant reminder to keep your chin up,
know who you are, and walk boldly forward.

Characters and Incidentals

Assassin's Mace - The supreme weapon. Not even certain to exist, its possibility deemed little more than a fiction, a peasant's tale. It was Di Xin who forged it into reality. He started first with a mysterious orb, gifted to him by Daji, who in turn became his wife. The orb had the property to seemingly capture and hold souls, or to wither the life force from who or whatever it touched. But intended users could not figure how to safely hold or wield it, so it had little use on the battlefield. Was there a solution? The quest commenced, but with little progress until a long-time prophecy came to fulfillment. One sinister evening a dragon-like creature lit the night skies of Shang in flame and culminated the spectacle planting a presumed dragon's egg onto the surface below. This proved to be the solution, as eventually Di Xin, exploiting the skills of the captive sage Jiang Ziya, merged the egg and the orb into its mace-like final form. Hence the Assassin's Mace. Whoever possessed it held power over life and death. A weapon supreme over all others, capable of stealing the life essence of one's enemies, disappearing them to time's end.

Bao Ling - "The Dragon of the Midlands." Protagonist around whom many of our stories revolve. Raised in a remote agrarian community, he opted to resist oppression, taking up arms to defend the weak and helpless. Branded as an outlaw and revolutionary and constantly on the run, he came upon a mysterious stranger, Sying Hao, who offered sanctuary on Southern Mountain. The bargain soon proved to extend far beyond the promised protection. Sying Hao became his mentor, and teacher, honing all of his talents and abilities to their highest realization. In some ways Bao Ling is everyman … just trying to make sense of the unknowable and the uncertain, while preserving his connections to the simple life of his forbears, and to the land and people he loves.

Bo Yikao - Oldest son of King Wen and brother to Wu Ji (King Wu). As surety of Zhou's fealty to Shang, hoping to ensure the continued safety of the Zhou state, Bo Yikao acquiesced to the summons of Di Xin and Daji requiring his detention in their palace. His stately presence, charisma, and talent soon became a distraction for Daji, and did not sit well with Di Xin. In the end, both considered the prince to be an extravagance best excised, fearing he might be the one who could turn Zhou into a troublesome rival state. Ignoring repercussions, they decided simply better to do away with him. History reports he is the first to have died the death of a thousand cuts, presumably the work of Daji … King Wen heard only his son had run off with a consort and had disappeared in shame. It proved a great miscalculation on Daji's part. King Wen, already an old man and deemed too feeble to embolden Zhou only seemed to grow stronger as he aged, as did the state of Zhou under his guiding influence over the decades which followed.

Colonel Sun (Sun Wu Kong) – Here, we encounter Sun nearly a millennium before he achieves distinction as honored officer and counselor in the service of Liu Bei. Close comrade to Zhuge Liang and colleague to Guan Yu. Mentor and fatherly influence on Sying Hao. Possibly an immortal, possibly a descendant of a distinct species. Forever shrouded in mystery. In no small part due to his guarded and reticent demeanor, barely offsetting his foreboding and ever solemn presence. His life and deeds linger as monuments preserved in legend and enshrined as myth. Directly, or indirectly, his influence and spirit sift throughout our tales and seem to ripple through the ages. We speak of him at considerable length over the course of many accounts and recollections.

Daji - (1076-1046 BCE) Wife to Di Xin; Queen of Shang. A fearless, wicked and immensely talented foil and counterpart to King Di Xin. Possessing a rare and unearthly beauty, she exploited her remarkable talents and gifts to sate an unyielding lust for power. Known as well for her inclination to perversion and sexual extravagance, she had once been a skilled assassin, sent at first to Kill King Di—but instead found in him a life partner both in love and depravity, both brazenly given to favor venal displays of sadism before all in the royal surrounds. Hearing of her escapades, commoners deemed her to be a witch, or a human possessed by a sinister fox spirit.

Danfu - Ji Danfu (Duke Danfu). Grandfather to King Wen. Rather than war unnecessarily with primitive neighboring communities, he led his people into the Wei River wilderness where they created a self-sufficient community. From this humble start, they became the State of Zhou. He prophesied the rising kingdom would become strong and prominent under his son and grandson. He further dreamt his grandson would one day happen upon a great sage; one whose beneficial influence on the family's destiny would be profound.

Di Xin - (1105-1046 BCE) King Di ... often referred to pejoratively as King Zhou of Shang; reign of 29 years; ascended at age 30. Degenerate last emperor of the Shang Dynasty. His subjects concluded his wife Daji ... because of her wanton and flagrant inclinations toward excess and depravity was a witch or possessed by a fox spirit. At first, a brilliant monarch and skilled logician, as well as martial artist … said to go after animals barehanded when on the hunt; he inexplicably turned to darkness. In our portrayal, his character changes radically after a failed coup and attempt on his life; mounted by his closest officers and staff. Isolated and trusting no one, he loses the will to live, or to rule. What emerges, largely influenced by Daji … who, alone, pulls him from his dismal depression, in time becomes a truly wicked monarch. Under her influence and inducement, he discovers evil to be the great elixir for personal liberation. For the balance of his reign, he devotes all of his energies to the perpetuation of evil and fear as the manifestation of his "art." There are no limits or constraints as he pushes relentlessly along this path in pursuit of his "masterpiece." Judged by history to be the very embodiment of evil and vile corruption, in folklore, he becomes the god of sodomy after his death.

Dragon's Egg - see Assassin's Mace

Fa Miu - "Old Fox." He is a character appearing in several of our tales. A practical, gifted, and worldly-wise gentleman, he often appears at first to be slave to whatever system or scheme he serves. Yet somehow he always manages to function independently. His true nature is excellence, and his aim inevitably directed toward the common good. We first meet him in *Seed of Dragons*, where he is a shadow principal shaping events, a true and fearless, though unsung hero. In *Token Tales and Fragments*, we find him at the other end of life, as the elder of two toll collectors encountered by Bao Ling on entering Fortune's Gateway. At first glance, a fox faced, world-wise and very clever old man, seemingly relegated to obscurity, bemoaning his fate, but adept at working within its limitations. He makes a quick and lasting impression on the young archer.

Guan Yu - (160-220 CE). Also referred to as Guan Gong (Lord Guan), or simply Guan. Sworn brother to Liu Bei and Zhang Fei (bound three as one by their Peach Garden Oath). Virtually peerless among human warriors. Revered as a staunch patron of righteousness. Protector of the oppressed, guardian of the weak and vulnerable. Particularly the Shu tribes, in whom he took an unshakable personal interest. In the lineage of our accounts, he becomes companion and peer to Sun Wu Kong (Colonel Sun). He is the only human ever considered by Sun Wu Kong to be his martial equal. In his prime, with no more than his Green Dragon Blade in hand, Guan Yu could alone, stand down an entire enemy army.

He Ling - Paternal Grandfather to Bao Ling. Of considerable influence in shaping his character and developing his unique talents. Though only a passing reference in this account, he connects through bloodline to a history of mysterious influences which only become apparent to Bao Ling as his own journey into uncertainty and challenge continues.

Iron Hand Gao - Friend of He Ling, Bao Ling's grandfather. Martial and life tutor to the child Bao Ling. Mentioned here only in a passing reference. A master of iron-hand and the internal disciplines and revered as benefactor and protector of his village and surrounds. Through direct example, he embodied the eternal awareness of life's direct connection to death, making clear for Bao Ling that how others want for us to think of them, may not be in fact what they are. Though their time together had been short due to harsh necessity, the impact of his character on shaping Bao Ling had been profound. After encountering a man like Iron Hand Gao, one is unlikely to fear any other, or anything else for that matter.

Jiang Yi - Daughter of Jiang Ziya. Respecting the final wishes of his father, King Wu took Jiang Yi as wife (r. 1046–1043 BC), establishing blood ties between the two renowned clans.

Jiang Ziya - nie Lü Shang - (11th century BCE). Had spent twenty years in the court of Di Xin, considered even then to be a great military mind. Because of his proven talents, and in spite of his loyalty, he lost favor with Di Xin. Deemed a threat to Di Xin, he convincingly feigned madness to avoid certain execution. Convinced of his madness but respecting a favor rendered, Di Xin had him released to his own devices whereupon he wandered alone into the wilderness. Said to have been seventy-two years old, seeming mindlessly to be fishing without a hook and bait when first discovered by King Wen. King Wen's own grandfather had once foretold the eventual encounter with a great sage in King Wen's dire moment of need. As adviser to King Wen, Jiang espoused the need to love the people one rules, and to serve their well-being, and never enrich oneself from their toils and suffering. On his advice, King Wen lowered the burden of taxation on the people and ended the practice of corvée labor. The effect on Zhou marked its rapid growth to prominence as a western state in the Shang empire. A philosopher and strategist of singular renown, Jiang's treatise on military strategy, "Six Secret Strategic Teachings," ranks as one of the Seven Military Classics of Ancient China. In the rarest combination of talents, he stands with the greatest of strategists, and humanists. History credits him as grand architect in the ascent of Zhou and catalyst to the eventual overthrow of Shang by King Wu. Within the context of our tale, he is a human who has accessed the secrets of immortality. Already an old man in appearance, he is indeed far older in fact. Historians record his time as (1128-1015 BCE; 113 years).

Ji Chang - See "King Wen."

Ji Li - King Ji; no dates; son of Duke Danfu the legendary founder of Zhou; Sima Qian recorded that he and his son were both renowned for their wisdom and this reputation caused Ji Li's elder brothers Taibo and Zhongyong to voluntarily renounce their claims on the throne and leave in self-exile to Wu (not the same "Wu" which became a state under the family Sun), entrusting free rein over the affairs of Zhou to their talented sibling. While nurturing his young state, Ji Li maintained a delicate balance of loyalty and fealty to Shang, while ever pushing the wellbeing of his own people and the development of his young domain. What sealed the deal for Zhou's survival was Ji Li's great martial talents, and as a vassal general in the service of Shang, he secured their western frontier. But then, the Shang leadership read his prowess as a potential threat, particularly since they had no counters should he turn against them. In the end, King Wen Ding of Shang betrayed his loyal vassal, engineering an elaborate scheme to have him eliminated.

King Cheng - Song Ji; ruled as King Cheng of Zhou (1042 to 1021 BCE). See Song Ji.

King Wen - King Wen (Ji Chang); lived 1152-1056 (96 years); ruled 1099–1050 BCE (49 years). The helmsman who steered the young state of Zhou unerringly to its destiny. It had been his dream to be the one who toppled the Shang … but wisely, he resisted the temptation to act before the time was right. While it was his son Wu who conquered the Shang following the Battle of Muye, King Wen was honored posthumously as the founder of the Zhou dynasty. A large number of the hymns in the Classic of Poetry are praises to the legacy of King Wen. Some consider him the first epic hero of Chinese history. He had mastered and refined the ancient arts of prognostication and receives credit for steering and delivering the "Yi Ching" into its modern form. He is grandson to Duke Danfu, founder of Zhou.

King Wu - King Wu; Wu Ji; Ji Fa (Son of King Wen) Reign 1046-1043 BCE; brother to Bo Yikao; and successor to King Wen. Wu seems to have been the agent of history and change. His unique and singular talents culminated a family chronicle of sacrifice and loss leaving no options to open revolt if their subsidiary state of Zhou were to survive. After the death of Bo Yikao, the course of Zhou veered to one of certain collision with Shang. No other man could have guided the overmatched state of Zhou to its decisive victory over the Shang. Standing high in the pantheon of heroes, his own life ended all too prematurely. Upon his demise, his brothers Guanshu, Caishu and Huoshu incited the rebellion of The Three Guards … countered by another brother, Duke Dan (Dan Ji, brother #4 vs. Guan Shu, brother #3). History remembers Duke Dan as the Duke of Zhou, a paragon of virtue, wisdom and humility.

Li Fung - "Master Li" of the Mountain People. Village elder. Martial master. He figures prominently in the personal development of Shi-Hui Ke, both as child, and as man. In our book *Seed of Dragons*, we give full account of the man and the considerable influence he has over his people. Now he is older. His one-time protege, Shi-Hui Ke, stands nearly his equal in the high esteem of the mountain tribes.

Liu Bei - (unknown 161 – 10 June 223 CE). The incomparable man of righteousness. A common man, though distant relation to the Han emperor. A sandal maker who rose to prominence as a formidable military commander—driven by his unsparing dedication to restoration of the Han Dynasty. Retreating to save what remained of his forces, he founded the Shu Han empire in the remote west, and prospered beyond all expectations— his achievements the stuff of dreams and legends. Until his demise, he remained a key principal during the period of the Three Kingdoms. He felt the Shu tribes to be a most noble and honorable people, believing that so long as they remained viable, there would be no direct path for Cao Cao and Wei to attack from the east. To that end, he ensured the Shu remained independent, and always, a respected ally. He nurtured, encouraged, and taught them how to fend for themselves.

Liu Shan - (207-271 CE); son of Liu Bei; ascended throne at age sixteen on the death of his father; initially under the charge of Chancellor Zhuge Liang; courtesy name - Gungsi; reign of 40 years longest of all in the Three Kingdom era. His name resonates even today, often used to describe one who lacks sense or ambition, or who would not achieve anything even with significant assistance. Surrendered to Wei 263 CE. Few specifics are known of his court and reign as Zhuge Liang banned official historians, leaving no formal record.

Red Hare - Many during that era regarded Red Hare to be the greatest warrior's horse ever to grace the battlefield. Chroniclers record he could cover five hundred li in a day, and that he never even broke stride ascending mountains, or crossing deserts. In battle, he moved forever forward, fearless, and completely attuned to his master. His coat glistened red, not a single hair of any other shade. When he moved in battle, the sweaty sheen on his coat took on a light of its own, casting a red glow on the faces of all those who closed to do him harm. A colored beam shaded blood red. You might say he was among horses, what Guan Yu was among men. At first, wild and intractable, Cao Cao gifted the creature to Guan Yu. A match destined; each completed the other. From the first meeting, they became inseparable.

Shi-Hui Ke - One of the Shu Mountain people. Abbot of Crystal Springs temple, a mysterious preserve and one of several fortresses meticulously conceived by Zhuge Liang to secure the Shu Roads from invasion. Created, in accordance with Liu Bei's directive, to protect and preserve the culture and heritage of the mountain people. Although a monk and man of peace, Shi-Hui Ke remains an ardent patriot, and has found purpose in his role as defender of his people and their ways. In his youth, he had attained renown as a singularly gifted martial artist, particularly in archery, before losing his left arm midway from the shoulder resulting from an unlucky encounter with a sadistic band of Wei mercenaries. They removed his left thumb, assuring he could wield no bow. Gangrene set in, taking the arm. In some ways, the unfortunate loss of his arm proved a blessing … in time, the once consummate archer, now monk, found within his higher states of awareness, the secret of the "thought arrow." Bao Ling had opportunity to witness Abbot Hui's remarkable skill, projecting nothing but concentrated thought to strike and deter a stalking tiger. We present the full account in *The Wizard's Testament*. He also appears to have gained privy to the alchemy of longevity, or so concludes Bao Ling; but that's a different story.

Song Ji - (1055-1021 BCE) Prince Song Ji; King Cheng; son of Wu Ji and heir to the throne of King Wu. Wu died while Song Ji was not yet of age. As a child, he became King Cheng, under the regency assumed by his uncle Dan Ji (the Duke of Zhou). The regency lasted seven years. Served as ruler 1042-1021 BCE. Died 1021 BCE.

Sun Wu Kong - See "Colonel Sun."

Sying Hao - Mentor to Bao Ling. A onetime war orphan who became apprentice and adopted son to Sun Wu Kong. Friend of the Southlanders and archer supreme. Scholar of the classics and bow craftsman of singular caliber. Guided by Sun, he mastered the transformations, learned to project consciousness, and to move about undetected. Thought by many to be a ghost. Sometimes called "Fenghua Yan" (weathered rock), or "The Man from Southern Mountain."

Wen Ding - (1112-1102 BCE). Shang Dynasty king. Arranged for the murder of King Ji.

Wu Ji - See "King Wu."

Yama - "King Yama." A devil of sorts, or perhaps what we might think of as the incarnation of death. Presides over hell and is accountable for the life, death and transmigration of human souls. Keeps true the final ledger and ensures his fearsome legions bring the newly departed to their end judgment. Relishes chaos and induces strife. Enjoys his job, particularly the part where he gets to torment those deserving. Once, when confronted by the Creator for his evil doings, he defended himself most eloquently, arguing to the Creator, "Hey ... isn't this my job? Did you make me for any other purpose? Can you think of anyone who can do it better than me? Forgive me sire, but I fail to see where there is a problem." Convinced by his logic and impressed with his integrity, the Creator ordered his release declaring him free to go about his business unimpeded.

Zhang Fei - (unknown - died 221 CE). Sworn brother to Guan Yu and Liu Bei. Also, a singular warrior, one whom Guan Yu deemed his peer and often boasted of. Known for his uncontrollable temper, it proved to be his ultimate undoing when assassinated by his own men. But not until fulfilling a life of epic feats and undeniable heroism.

Zhuge Liang (181 - 234 CE) - Sometimes referred to as "Kongming" the Sleeping Dragon, attesting to the splendor of his essential nature once unleashed. A wizard, scholar, musician and hero whose influence and guiding hand threads either directly or indirectly throughout our accounts, and perhaps beyond them. Despite his many deeds of record, historical abstracts say little of his past, or his background. No one can account for how he gained his remarkable talents. For that reason, he remains an enigma. In our recitations, the dates of his life are indeterminate. He has achieved longevity; though, not having fully mastered its alchemy, he is not a true immortal. As a Merlin-like sage who has perfected awareness, he stands singular, and among humans and other creatures, is regarded with the same reverence as the likes of Jiang Ziya and Sun Wu Kong.

Acknowledgments

A work like this challenges one with numerous tasks, hurdles and twists - particularly the seemingly endless revisions and fine-tunings. Then there's the book cover, and the layout, required for both print and E-book. Life's usual demands don't quiet during the creative journey. Crises, illnesses, and daily distractions regularly threaten derailments. Someone once asked how many re-writes I do. I'll just say, a lot, and leave it at that. I usually stop counting at fifty.

Like most, I struggle with interruptions and losing focus. That's when I come to depend on others. Renee Knarreborg, a longtime friend and collaborator once again graced our effort with her artwork and insightful images. Renee devises her wonders while navigating regional power and utility issues and running audits.

Also, many thanks to friends and colleagues for their generosity in providing valuable feedback and insights which changed and improved the evolving work. They tackled whatever I cast their way with a relentless yet fair-minded passion, always aiming for excellence, clarity, and relevance. This work is undoubtedly better because of their kindness and commitment to excellence, all freely rendered while pushing through life challenges of their own.

Lastly, I am deeply grateful to the many mentors[23] and teachers who have guided me over the decades, sharing

---

[23] If you're curious, here's a link:
https://ironcrane.com/IC_Flowchart.jpeg

their wisdom and skills. Most have passed on, and I now stand in their shoes rather than on their shoulders. To those still with us, please accept my advance apologies for any fouls rendered. Whatever I got wrong is not your fault or doing.

About the Author

Billy Ironcrane was raised in inner city Philadelphia during the 1950's and 1960's. He partook in the revolutionary currents of change, protest, activism, and idealism which characterized the era. While a teen, he spent summers on the Jersey coast hawking newspapers, tossing burgers and exploring places like Atlantic City where he encountered flea circuses, Gene Krupa hanging between sets at the Steel Pier, petrified mermaids and the fabulously wealthy promenading the boardwalk at night flashing mink stoles, diamonds, tuxes and studded canes. Atlantic City dubbed itself, "The World's Playground." All the stuff of dreams as he returned to Mrs. J's boarding house where he slept for ten bucks a week, sharing occasional space with his grandfather and other Polish immigrants working the summer trade. Not to mention the landlady's ever-present legion of cats.

He departed the inner city still in his teens, and pushed blindly into the unknown never to return. There he found his many stories and mapped his own insights into the nature of existence. To remain static and have done nothing would have been terminal, as in fact it proved to be for many of his mates.

In the decades following, he pursued new awarenesses. He swam exotic currents, wandered through remote tropical forests, and became a soldier. He ambled through southwestern deserts at night, slept through thunderstorms alongside petrified forests, and trekked the Rockies. He mastered the martial arts, jogged with blacktail deer in the hills surrounding Monterey, explored Zen, and motorcycled the California coast. He scaled Pfeiffer Rock, freelanced, traversed the Cascades, and slept beneath ancient redwoods in remote Los Padres. Along the way, he raised a family and bridged the corporate jungle. Then, he hung a shingle and lived on wits and ingenuity until the muse of the 60's again tapped his shoulder, ordering, "Time to shift gears, Billy."

So there you have it.

Other Works by Billy Ironcrane

Returning to Center
(A Collection of Stories, Vignettes and Thoughts)

Seed of Dragons
(Surviving an Empire Undone)

Token Tales and Fragments
(Recalling a Time of Heroes and Sages)

The Wizard's Testament
(An Unexpected Challenge)

The Gift of Red Hare
(And Other Epic Tales)